— .✦. —

PRAISE FOR DONNA GRANT'S
BEST-SELLING ROMANCE NOVELS

— .✦. —

"Grant's ability to quickly convey complicated
backstory makes this jam-packed love story accessible
even to new or periodic readers."
—*Publishers' Weekly*

"Donna Grant has given the paranormal genre
a burst of fresh air…"
—*San Francisco Book Review*

"The premise is dramatic and heartbreaking; the characters are
colorful and engaging; the romance is spirited and seductive."
—*The Reading Cafe*

"The central romance, fueled by a hostage drama, plays
out in glorious detail against a backdrop of multiple ongoing
issues in the "Dark Kings" books. This seemingly penultimate
installment creates a nice segue to a climactic end."
—*Library Journal*

"…intense romance amid the growing
war between the Dragons and the
Dark Fae is scorching hot."
—*Booklist*

DRAGON KINGS® SERIES
Dragon Revealed ~ Dragon Mine
Dragon Unbound ~ Dragon Eternal
Dragon Lover ~ Dragon Arisen
Dragon Frost ~ Dragon Kiss ~ Dragon Born
Dragon Marked ~ Dragon Forged ~ Dragon Sieged

SKYE DRUIDS SERIES
Iron Ember ~ Shoulder the Skye ~ Heart of Glass
Endless Skye ~ Still of the Night ~ Blood Skye
After Midnight ~ Kiss of Skye

DARK KINGS SERIES
Dark Heat ~ Darkest Flame ~ Fire Rising
Burning Desire ~ Hot Blooded ~ Night's Blaze
Soul Scorched ~ Dragon King ~ Passion Ignites
Smoldering Hunger ~ Smoke and Fire
Dragon Fever ~ Firestorm ~ Blaze ~ Dragon Burn
Constantine: A History, Parts 1-3 ~ Heat ~ Torched
Dragon Night ~ Dragonfire ~ Dragon Claimed
Ignite ~ Fever ~ Dragon Lost ~ Flame ~ Inferno
A Dragon's Tale (Whisky and Wishes: *A Holiday Novella*,
Heart of Gold: *A Valentine's Novella*, and
Of Fire and Flame) ~ My Fiery Valentine
The Dragon King Coloring Book
Dragon King Special Edition
Character Coloring Book: Rhi

DARK WARRIORS SERIES
Midnight's Master ~ Midnight's Lover
Midnight's Seduction ~ Midnight's Warrior
Midnight's Kiss ~ Midnight's Captive
Midnight's Temptation ~ Midnight's Promise
Midnight's Surrender ~ A Warrior for Christmas

CHIASSON SERIES
Wild Fever ~ Wild Dream ~ Wild Need
Wild Flame ~ Wild Rapture

LARUE SERIES
Moon Kissed ~ Moon Thrall
Moon Struck ~ Moon Bound

WICKED TREASURES
Seized by Passion ~ Enticed by Ecstasy ~ Captured by Desire

◆

HISTORICAL PARANORMAL

THE KINDRED SERIES
Everkin ~ Eversong ~ Everwylde
Everbound ~ Evernight ~ Everspell

KINDRED: THE FATED SERIES
Rage ~ Ruin ~ Reign

DARK SWORD SERIES
Dangerous Highlander
Forbidden Highlander ~ Wicked Highlander
Untamed Highlander ~ Shadow Highlander
Darkest Highlander

ROGUES OF SCOTLAND SERIES
The Craving ~ The Hunger
The Tempted ~ The Seduced

THE SHIELDS SERIES
A Dark Guardian ~ A Kind of Magic
A Dark Seduction ~ A Forbidden Temptation ~ A Warrior's Heart
Mystic Trinity (a series connecting novel)

DRUIDS GLEN SERIES
Highland Mist ~ Highland Nights ~ Highland Dawn
Highland Fires ~ Highland Magic
Mystic Trinity (a series connecting novel)

SISTERS OF MAGIC TRILOGY
Shadow Magic ~ Echoes of Magic ~ Dangerous Magic

THE ROYAL CHRONICLES
NOVELLA SERIES
Prince of Desire ~ Prince of Seduction
Prince of Love ~ Prince of Passion
Mystic Trinity
(a series connecting novel)

**Check out Donna Grant's Online Store at
www.DonnaGrant.com/shop
for autographed books, character
themed goodies, and more!**

Dark Alpha's Temptation

NEW YORK TIMES & USA TODAY BESTSELLING AUTHOR

DONNA GRANT

www.DonnaGrant.com
www.MotherofDragonsBooks.com

Dark Alpha's Temptation

THE REAPERS

The seven there are, warriors all.
Do not do wrong or their blade will fall.
Their appearances shrouded.
Their approach, clouded.
Against evil they fight.
Power and magic are their might.
They serve only one.
If you expose their identity – run.
Secrecy is their defense.
If the truth escapes, Death will commence.

CHAPTER

one

Drumshanbo, Ireland
June

It was good to be right.

Then again, Kyra was always right. The pub was more crowded than usual, but she paid the patrons no attention as she tossed back the whisky and quietly set the empty glass on the bar before weaving her way through the people to the side door.

Her target didn't see her. Though she made a point of not being seen. It was a gift her aunt had taught her, and Kyra put the skill to good use. Still, she never imagined she'd use her talent to follow a Reaper.

She slipped out of the pub into the summer night. Drumshanbo might be a small village, but it was a mecca for travelers since it was perfectly situated and contained woodlands, rolling hills, and lakes, as well as the Iron Mountains.

The Reaper halted. Kyra ducked into a nearby alley and waited several seconds before she walked out as if she hadn't been following him. The Reaper was gone. This wasn't the first time she'd lost him, but she wasn't rattled by it at all.

Kyra sensed that she was being watched. No doubt by the Reaper himself. She inwardly smiled and walked to her motorbike. She strapped on her helmet and then put on her gloves before starting the engine. Something had brought the Reaper to Drumshanbo, and she was going to find out what it was.

She revved the engine before checking her blind spot and pulling out into traffic. It wasn't long before Kyra was out of the village and on the dark, winding roads. She pointed her motorbike toward the mountains. The cabin she'd chosen was out of the way, which meant that there was no reason for anyone to drive past it.

The truth was that she liked being at the top of the ridge. She enjoyed the view, but really, she liked that it reminded her of the stories her aunt used to tell her about the Fae Realm and all its wonders.

Kyra parked the bike next to the cottage and walked to the door. She paused, putting her hand against the edge of the door to feel for the wards she'd placed. They hadn't been disturbed. Her magic wasn't exceptionally strong, but she was able to do a multitude of things that other Fae couldn't. Besides, it didn't matter how strong her magic was because she doubted there would be anything that could keep a Reaper out if he wanted in badly enough.

She gave a little push with her magic, and the door opened, undoing both the human and the Fae locks. She set her helmet, gloves, and keys on the small table inside the door before she removed her jacket and raked her fingers through her hair. There was a bump against her leg before a meow reached her. Kyra leaned down and scratched the cat behind the ears. The tiny calico had shown up the first day Kyra arrived, and the animal had been coming around ever since. Kyra had no idea how the cat kept getting inside, but in truth, it was nice to return and find the animal there. Not that the cat stayed. Just long enough to eat, maybe get in a little nap, and then the calico was gone until the next day.

"Did you have a good day?" Kyra asked as she picked up the cat and walked into the kitchen.

The cat purred loudly, rubbing its head against Kyra's chin. She laughed as she got the can of cat food out of the cabinet. The cat jumped out of her arms and wound around Kyra's legs as she dished out the meal.

She set the dish down and squatted beside the animal as it began eating. "In case you were wondering, I had a pretty good day myself. I saw him again. I'm going to need to be more careful, though. I don't wish to anger him before I've had a chance to speak to him."

The cat looked up, blinking its big, green eyes at her.

Kyra twisted her lips. "You should see him. He's . . . well, let's just say he turns heads."

The cat licked her muzzle and simply stared.

Kyra rolled her eyes and straightened. "Fine. He's mouthwateringly gorgeous. Is that what you want me to say?"

In answer, the calico went back to eating.

Kyra sighed and walked to the desk. She spread out the pictures she'd taken of the Reaper. She didn't need the human contraption to remember his face, but she liked being able to stare at the photos of him. She wished she knew his name. He was tall and broad-shouldered and walked with a confidence that caused others to give him a wide berth. He used glamour to shield his eyes and hair around humans, but she had gotten to see his true coloring.

Deep crimson eyes that showed not an ounce of mercy. Black hair with silver weaved throughout the thick length that was longer on top and shorter on the sides.

She should be wary of him. Not only was he a Reaper, but he was also Dark. Those two things should've been all she needed to steer clear. Instead, she had found herself enraptured. Completely smitten.

Utterly infatuated.

It had been by pure accident that she'd even discovered there were Reapers. And if the seven of them—along with the one Dark female—hadn't been fighting a dozen pale-skinned creatures at the Light Castle, they would've noticed her. Thankfully, their attention had been on the beasts, which allowed her a view of the battle, something she'd likely never see again.

Kyra knew the face of all seven Reapers, but it was the one she followed that stood out to her. It had nothing to do with his kissable lips, penetrating eyes, or his amazing body. That was a lie she couldn't even tell herself. There had been something about the Reaper's face that had pulled at Kyra instantly.

Perhaps she would've had better luck following the female Dark with her long braids and red nails.

Kyra shook her head. The moment her eyes had landed on her Reaper, she hadn't been able to look away. He had fought like a wild man. He was savage and ferocious, and she hadn't been able to look at anyone or anything else. He hadn't given any quarter to the beasts. And Kyra had a feeling that her Reaper looked at the world just like that.

No quarter.

No forgiveness.

Her gaze ran over the face in the photo. Hollow cheeks, thin lips, regal nose, and a square jawline. It was a face she would never forget. It was also one she would never share with anyone else.

The Fae, in general, were terrified of the Reapers. Some didn't believe the Reapers were real, while others were wholeheartedly convinced of them. Like all Fae children, Kyra had been told the stories as a kid. She'd feared the Reapers for much of her life, but after a while, when she'd found no proof of them, that terror began to ebb.

It wasn't until the battle at the Light Castle that she realized the Reapers were real. Well, to be fair, she hadn't known who the seven warriors were at first, but it didn't take her long to piece it together.

The Dark female that battled with them? Well, that was another piece of the puzzle Kyra hadn't figured out yet. She would eventually, but right now, her attention was on her Reaper and finding out everything she could about him.

It was dangerous. She knew that, but there wasn't much about her life that wasn't. She'd been living on the fringes of the Fae world for centuries now, interacting with both sides and gaining information she could pass on. Most times, she dealt more with the humans, but she still made sure to get to the Light Castle often to keep up with what was going on with the Fae.

The castle was a hub of information for the Light. All Kyra had to do was hang out there for a few hours, and she was able to learn all kinds of juicy gossip. Most of it was nonsense, but she always came away with a gem or two.

She set the photo down and leaned back in the chair to prop her feet up on the edge of the desk. Her mother had wanted her to be a proper lady. It was expected of any female in their family line, but Kyra had rebelled. She'd wanted to go her own way. Her father had humored her, but her mother had fought her on every little thing until Kyra couldn't take it anymore.

That's when her aunt stepped in. Eva had gone through something very similar to Kyra, so her aunt had decided to take matters into her own hands. It was Eva who made sure that Kyra kept a relationship with her parents. It was also Eva who'd taught her how to embrace what made her different, but also to accept and love what made her part of their family.

Kyra missed Eva deeply. Her aunt had gone missing over a century ago. It wasn't like Eva at all, which is why Kyra had known that something was wrong. But no matter where she looked, no matter who she asked, no one had any answers. It was like Eva had just stopped existing one day.

There were answers, and Kyra was going to find them. There was a chance that the Reapers might know something. It was a long shot, but at this point, Kyra was reaching for anything. If only she could learn more about the Reapers before she approached them. There was very little to go on, though, and even less that anyone knew.

She had asked around and got a different answer about the Reapers from nearly everyone she spoke with. No one seemed to know anything for sure. And since she was the only Light who had somehow managed to see the battle with the creatures, no one knew what she was talking about.

Kyra dropped her feet to the floor and rose. She walked to the bathroom and stared at her reflection. She ran her fingers through her long hair, using magic to shift the green locks to a light pink. As a final touch, she changed the length, altering it to chin-length with the right side shaved.

No matter what hairstyle or color she tried, she had yet to find anything she kept for more than a day. It also prevented others from recognizing her, which was a big help when she was trailing a Reaper who had keen senses.

She really wished she knew his name.

More than that, she wanted to know what it was about him that drew her.

"A Dark and a Reaper." Kyra shook her head at her reflection. "Yeah. That's real smart. Eva would kick your ass into next month for being so dumb."

The smile died as her mind drifted once more to her aunt. Kyra pushed away from the sink and walked outside to stand beneath the night sky. There was something calming about looking at the stars. She stayed there for a long time, thinking of the past and the path she found herself on now. She hoped the Reapers had resources she didn't to locate Eve, because she was willing to do whatever was necessary to find her family.

With a sigh, Kyra went back inside to the bedroom. She removed her boots and clothes and slipped into a short gown made of white silk. Then she lay on the bed. She gazed up at the ceiling, her mind going over everything from that day. Her Reaper had seemed to be searching for something. Or someone. He didn't talk to anyone, just walked the streets and occasionally went into a pub, though he never stayed long.

She could have lost his trail at any time. So far, he'd been relatively easy to find, going from one village to the next. But how long would that last? Maybe it was time that she approached him. What harm would it do to talk to him?

She scrunched up her face at the thought. It was probably the worst idea she'd ever had. Only second to the one where she'd decided to follow him in the first place.

Kyra had seen him fight. She knew exactly what he was capable of and how quickly he moved. No doubt he had other skills she didn't know about. That had led her to wonder how long she could follow him without him knowing. She was good, but he was a Reaper.

Kyra blew out a breath. The best thing would be for her to forget her Reaper. To let him go his way as she went another. Yeah. That would be the smart thing to do.

But she wouldn't.

She knew it with the same certainty that she knew she would never own a pair of high heels. There were just some things that weren't her—and giving up was one of them.

Though her real motivation for trailing her Reaper was to get answers, that wasn't all of it. In fact, she was pretty sure she was following him simply because she couldn't stop following him.

"Oh, Mum would just love hearing that," she told herself with a roll of her eyes.

If only she could find a reliable source to tell her more about the Reapers. She wanted details. All the details. Especially about one Dark Reaper with large hands and broad shoulders and red eyes she couldn't stop thinking about.

She closed her eyes as her body pulsed with desire, a need that went soul-deep. It was the same each time she thought about him. It had happened the first time she saw him, as well. Like some switch had been flipped the moment her gaze landed on him.

Almost as if she had . . . come alive . . . at the sight of him. All she thought about was him. And her dreams? The things he did to her in her fantasies made her tremble with need.

Kyra rolled onto her side and tried to ignore her body, but she knew it was useless. There would be no sleep until she gave herself some relief. The hunger would be back in the morning, but at least she would have a few hours of respite.

She flopped onto her back and let thoughts of her Reaper fill her mind as her hand drifted between her legs.

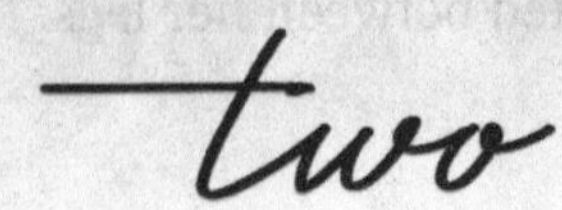

two

He was being followed. Dubhan was sure of it. He'd spent the better part of the day putting himself in positions where he could get a look at whoever it was.

It had taken him longer than he wanted to admit, but once he realized that the woman kept changing her hair and eyes but not her features, he was able to find her. He was shocked that she hadn't used glamour for her face or her body.

Dubhan had wanted to confront her, but he'd decided to hold off. She must have known he suspected her because she had left the area on a motorbike soon after. He was intrigued as to why she wouldn't use her magic to teleport away, but that wasn't the only thing that fascinated him.

It hadn't taken him long to locate the Fae after she rode off. He stood outside the small cottage on top of the mountain. Everything she did reminded him of a human—almost as if she would prefer to be one rather than a Fae.

More disturbing was why she followed him. For some reason, she had picked him out, but he couldn't figure out why or how. As a Reaper, he could veil himself indefinitely. Yet that didn't seem to deter the female.

In fact, she had managed to locate him despite his attempts to throw her off. It was like she had somehow found a way to link herself to him. But that was impossible.

Wasn't it?

He peered in the window as she walked through the house. It wasn't long before she came out of the bathroom with her hair changed again. The wild colors and styles should make her stand out, but in a world where humans experimented with all kinds of hair color, she fit right in.

Dubhan took a step toward the door to confront her, but then he hesitated. He didn't want to get involved in whatever this female was doing. There were other important matters to attend to, namely getting a location on Xaneth.

Though, if Dubhan were honest, he suspected that the royal Light Fae was dead, and that Usaeil, the Light Queen, had somehow managed to make sure that Death—and thereby the Reapers—couldn't locate his body.

Dubhan blew out a breath. Everything was so fekked up. With Usaeil now dead, things should have returned to normal, but he was beginning to think that wasn't going to happen.

The Light weren't the only ones without a ruler. The Dark were also floundering since Balladyn, their king, had been slain by none other than Usaeil. Dubhan had liked Balladyn, mainly because he had done great things for the Dark in the short amount of time he'd sat on the throne.

"Fekking Usaeil," Dubhan mumbled angrily.

The Light Queen had fooled everyone, but most especially her own people. The Light didn't know what to do with the fact that the queen they had followed for eons had been Dark nearly the entire time.

No one knew what to do about the Fae. Death was nothing more than judge and jury for their souls, and the Reapers were the executioners for Death. If Erith had foreseen any of this, she hadn't told them. Then again, Death didn't tell them much.

Dubhan ran a hand down his face. No matter how intrigued he was by the female in the cottage, there were bigger things at stake right now. Though it felt as if the chaos was getting out of hand.

For the Reapers, nothing had changed. One group of seven still reaped souls for Death, while Dubhan's group continued their search for Xaneth. There was only one fact they knew— Usaeil had taken her nephew. No one knew if Xaneth was dead, if Usaeil had changed him into one of her Trackers, or if Xaneth was being kept somewhere.

Though Dubhan was veiled, he still froze the minute the female looked out her window in his direction, his thoughts scattering as he focused on her. She couldn't see him, of that he was sure. Yet, he felt her eyes on him. He'd been veiled in the midst of hundreds of others who looked right through him, and he'd never experienced the like before.

Who was this Fae?

The question kept running through his mind. He gave a shake of his head. He could leave right then, go to a different part of the world or even another realm, and end whatever it was this female attempted to do by following him.

Yet, he didn't move.

Something kept him rooted to the spot. Was it the female? Was it the fact that he'd searched Drumshanbo for a couple of days but remained because something told him he might find a clue that lead to Xaneth?

He wished he had some answers because then he might not feel so disoriented. The female walked out of the house and came to stand on the porch. She wrapped her arms around herself and lifted her face as she closed her eyes. She stood there for several minutes, simply being.

Dubhan couldn't remember the last time he had done anything close to that. For as far back as he could remember, his life had been filled with one mission after another—before he died, and after.

He couldn't take his eyes off her. She was tall, her form shapely. She had a heart-shaped face with eyes that pierced whatever they landed on as if she had to absorb whatever it was she looked at. She had a wide mouth, her lips on the thin side but incredibly sexy. Especially when she smiled, which she did often.

And she gave it freely. From Fae to humans, and even to animals. There was a happy quality to her that Dubhan couldn't quite understand. The majority of all Fae—both Dark and Light— were in a state of shock at the moment, everyone trying to figure out what to do and who would rule.

Fighting would begin soon between factions, where each sought to take a throne. Would she get swept up in it? Dubhan sincerely hoped not. He didn't want anything to dull her smile. It made her . . . unique.

Like now. She simply enjoyed the peace and the sounds that filled the night around her. Dubhan let his lids fall closed. Then he lifted his face to the sky.

At first, all he heard were the animals. Then he felt the breeze upon his cheek. It tickled him a bit, causing him to grin. He took a deep breath and inhaled the fragrance of the flowers all around him, bringing in yet another of his senses.

The tension began to leave his limbs as he stood in the moonlight, soaking up everything around him. He didn't know how long he stood there before he realized that he could hear something else. It was faint, like something beating.

His attention lowered to the ground beneath his feet. And he realized that he was feeling, hearing, and sensing the magic within the realm.

He'd always known it was there, but this was the first time Dubhan had actually felt it. It penetrated through skin, muscle, and bone to sink into his soul. It was such a profound moment that it took his breath away.

His eyes snapped open. He wanted—no, he needed—to share the experience with someone. When he looked to where the female stood, she was gone. He was alone in the midst of an experience unlike any other, and he had no one to share it with.

He could tell the other Reapers, but how could he explain something that he himself didn't truly understand? But he knew the female would.

Dubhan squatted down and put his hand upon the earth that was still warm from the sun. He pushed magic into the soil, giving back to the realm what it gave to every magical being who lived upon it.

When Dubhan straightened, he didn't feel so disconnected anymore. If anything, it seemed as if he were strengthened. He wasn't as weary either. He felt rejuvenated.

He took two steps before he stopped. Dubhan turned back to the house. He thought about teleporting inside, but he suspected there were spells and wards up. They wouldn't keep him out, but they would alert her that he was there.

While he wanted to know who she was, he decided another approach might be beneficial. A plan took root. He shot one last look at the cottage before he returned to the village to continue his search for Xaneth.

Something was keeping him in Drumshanbo. He needed to figure out what it was and discover if it had anything to do with Xaneth. He remained veiled as he walked the streets, looking inside buildings, watching others, and listening to conversations.

He spotted two Fae—a Light male and a Dark female—who attempted to make it look as if they were casually meeting up when it was anything but.

"Were you followed?" the male asked.

The woman shook her head. "You?"

He shot her a flat look. "Everyone is so freaked out that no one in my family even noticed I was gone."

"It's that bad, huh?" she asked.

The male blew out a breath and nodded. "No one knows what to believe. The queen is dead, Inen is nowhere to be found, most of the Queen's Guard has been decimated, and there is division within the Light as people start to make it known they could lead."

"That doesn't sound as bad as the Dark," the female replied. "Balladyn had begun to make us trust, and within hours after his death, it's all gone to shite. If someone doesn't take the throne soon, the Dark could implode."

"Damn. I had no idea."

"The same thing could happen to the Light."

"What the hell happened to us? We were once a people to be feared and respected, and now. . . ."

He trailed off, but Dubhan didn't need to hear the rest. He

understood exactly what the male was saying. The once-great Fae had been brought to their knees. It would take someone special to pick them back up again.

Dubhan didn't know who would be the right person to lead the Dark. But the Light? Well, he suspected that Death had been eyeing someone for quite some time—Rhi.

Erith had taken a special interest in the Light Fae, but she would never tell anyone why. It was Death who had told Rhi it was her job to take out Usaeil. Rhi had done it, but at what cost? Rhi had seen Balladyn, her friend and ally, cut down in front of her by the queen.

It hadn't taken much effort for Dubhan to see the darkness growing within Rhi. Balladyn must have seen it, as well. The King of the Dark could have used that to his advantage and turned Rhi since he was in love with her. Perhaps it was because Balladyn loved Rhi that he hadn't done that.

Regardless, Rhi killing Usaeil and putting a stop to the queen's quest to take over both the Light and Dark had taken more out of Rhi than anyone expected. If Erith had predicted that Rhi would take the Light throne, then it seemed Death was wrong.

The thing was, Erith was never wrong.

So, what had happened?

Dubhan left the two Fae to continue their conversation. There might come a time when the Reapers had to step in and sort things out. Death could take over as queen since she was, in fact, a goddess, but being Queen of the Fae wasn't something she wanted.

He continued to think about the goings-on of the Light and Dark Fae as he wandered the streets. He noticed that his meanderings kept bringing him by a nondescript building. One that had been around for over three hundred years. He had walked past it numerous times over the last two days.

Dubhan halted before it and stared. The sign read that it was a bookstore. The building itself had been repaired, showing no signs of dereliction. He walked to the door and started to touch it when he noticed the marking on the doorway. It was one meant to keep Fae out.

And right below it was another symbol that he had seen only once before—etched on the doorframe of his family's home.

CHAPTER
three

She wondered if the Reaper knew that he stood out like a sore thumb amid the plain humans. Kyra hid a smile when she noticed those nearest the Reaper staring at him with blatant interest, but he paid them no attention.

Kyra got as close to him as she dared as they walked along the street. He had occupied her thoughts all night. Actually, he'd taken up residence in her mind since she had first seen him. It was reckless for her to get so close, but she couldn't seem to help herself. He was like a magnet, and she was helpless to resist his pull. It might get her killed, but even knowing that, she still maneuvered her way near him.

It wasn't until only one person separated them that she decided she was close enough. His stride was easy as he moved along the sidewalk. If he realized there was a group of people around him, he didn't act as if it mattered. Some stayed by him for a little while before they moved on. Others never left him, not even when he walked into shops.

And Kyra was one of those.

She sidled into the pub and took a seat before the Reaper made it to the bar. Oddly, he looked more at ease today than he had previously. Something must have happened after she'd left him yesterday. It made Kyra wish she had stuck around to see what he had found. Whatever it was, she bet it was interesting.

Or maybe her life was just so damn boring that she had to latch on to someone else.

No, that wasn't it at all. This was a Reaper! A real Reaper. And she was going to learn all she could about him while she had the chance. He hadn't taken a second look at her today, which meant that he didn't recognize her. Changing her hairstyle and color, as well as her eyes, seemed to do the trick. It was strange that her wild hair color didn't make her stand out, but when so many others had shades of blue, purple, green, orange, pink, and everything in between, she fit right in.

Kyra ordered a drink and glanced out the window. It made her feel less stalkery when she looked away from the Reaper every now and again. When the waitress arrived with her drink, Kyra glanced at the bar, but the Reaper was gone. Kyra hastily searched the pub without making it too obvious. She didn't see him, so she got up with her beer and walked toward the dart boards in a bid to take a better look around.

It was then that she noticed the hallway leading to the toilets. No doubt he was in there. She licked her lips and decided to return to her table to see if he came back out or not. Kyra pivoted and jerked as she found him standing right behind her, his eyes locked on her.

"I'm curious to know why you've been following me."

His voice was deep, his Irish accent thick. She realized, belatedly, that she hadn't heard him speak before that moment. She grasped something else, as well. She liked his voice. A lot. It slid over her like honey, thick, seductive, and all-consuming.

A brow quirked on his handsome face. Kyra blinked then, comprehending that she hadn't answered him. Wait. What was the question? She frowned as she tried to remember his words. That's right. He wanted to know why she was following him.

Her eyes widened as it hit her. Shite. He'd known!

"An answer would be really good now," he said in a no-nonsense tone.

Kyra swallowed, deciding it was better to go with a partial truth—all the while, hoping he believed her. "I can't seem to help myself."

"That isn't an answer."

She licked her lips and shrugged.

"You aren't telling me everything."

She hated to admit that he was right, but then again, she didn't want to tell him everything. She wasn't quite sure what he would do when he learned it all.

He sighed loudly and put his hand on her lower back to guide her toward a booth in the back corner. He slid into one side, and Kyra took the other. She set her pint of ale down, grateful not to have to hold it anymore since she couldn't seem to stop shaking.

She'd suspected that he would confront her one day, but she hadn't actually gotten around to thinking about what she would say when that happened, so she was ill-prepared for any of this. Though that was possibly the stupidest thing ever since preparing to talk to the Reaper should have been the first thing she'd done.

"Let's start with something easy," he said as he laid his arms on the table. "Your name."

"Kyra. Kyra Kavanaugh."

He nodded. "That wasn't too hard, was it?"

She found herself grinning. "Do I get your name?"

He hesitated a moment, then said, "Dubhan."

"Dubhan," she repeated, liking how it rolled off her tongue. The name meant dark or black, and since he was a Dark Fae, it suited him. But also because she could sense there was something he carried with him, like demons he couldn't quite shake that hung over him like a gloomy cloud.

"Now, how about you start at the beginning?"

She glanced at the table. "Only if I have your assurance you won't harm me."

"Harm you?" His face contorted with a frown as if her very words had offended him. "I have no reason to harm you."

"I want your assurance first," she insisted.

He stared at her for a long minute before he nodded. "I give you my word, I won't harm you."

"Nor will anyone you know harm me."

He narrowed his eyes. "I know a lot of people."

Yeah, that was probably too much to ask. "I had to try."

Dubhan sat back, his hands folded on the table as he patiently waited.

Kyra took a deep breath and said, "I saw you at the Light Castle."

He didn't so much as bat an eye.

So, she decided to reveal a bit more. "I saw you, the Dark female, and six others like you battling those strange creatures."

He moved so fast she didn't have time to react. One moment they were sitting in the pub. The next, he'd grasped her arm and teleported them to a thick forest. Kyra tried to jerk her arm free, but his grip didn't loosen.

"You're mistaken," he stated in a firm tone.

She glared at him, raising her chin. "I'm not lying, nor am I mistaken. I know what I saw. I don't know why no one else at the castle witnessed it, but I certainly did."

"Tell me all you saw," he demanded. His entire body was taut, his nostrils flaring as he stared at her.

Kyra tried to teleport away, but she couldn't leave. Whether it was his grip or their location, she was stuck with him. And that wasn't a good thing.

"Kyra," he growled.

She glanced down at his hand on her arm. "Release me."

"Not until you tell me what I want to know."

"There isn't much to tell. I was outside when the first creature appeared. It wasn't until the two women and the creature began fighting that I crouched down behind some bushes to hide and possibly try to help if they needed—which I might add, they didn't. I never had time to get away before the other creatures came."

"You were in Aisling's shield," he murmured as he looked away.

She leaned closer. "What?"

His gaze snapped back to her. "Nothing."

"Who's Aisling? Is she the one with the braids?"

"It doesn't matter," he told her. "Have you been following me ever since?"

Well, now, that really did make her sound like a stalker. Kyra shrugged half-heartedly. "Not every second. You did leave the Light Castle."

He let go of her so quickly, she stumbled back a step. He crossed his arms over his chest, and his gaze narrowed, telling her that he wasn't buying her words at all. "And you just happened to be in Drumshanbo the same time as me?"

Kyra hesitated, unsure if she should tell him more.

"That's what I thought," he muttered and rolled his eyes. Then he flattened his lips. "I think you ought to tell me the rest."

"You don't want to know."

"I really don't, but I have to. You can either tell me, or you can tell my friends."

Ugh. When given those options, she didn't have much choice. She glanced away, wondering if she could get free. Then she realized that she was talking to a Reaper, the very thing she had hoped to do. It just wasn't going like she wanted it to. "After that battle, I realized I had witnessed Reapers."

"For fek's sake," he muttered under his breath and dropped his chin to his chest.

Kyra paused, wondering if she had gotten it wrong. Maybe he wasn't a Reaper. Then she shook her head. No, Dubhan was definitely a Reaper. "I did some digging on the Reapers," she continued. "There isn't much information out there, and what is, doesn't really say anything. Nor will anyone tell me anything about your group."

He kept his head down as he asked, "How did you find me?"

"I honestly don't know. I kept thinking about you, and the next thing I knew, you were there. It's how it's been ever since."

"Thinking about me?" he asked, his head lifting to meet her gaze. "Me?"

Kyra nodded, realizing how insane she probably sounded.

"What do you want from me?"

"Nothing," she replied hastily, deciding to put off asking about her aunt for the moment since Dubhan seemed so . . . irritated. "I just want to get to know you."

He took a step toward her, dropping his arms to his sides. "That's dangerous, Kyra. More than you can possibly imagine."

"You said you wouldn't harm me."

He shook his head and glanced at the sky. "Some things are out of my control. And there are rules."

That all but confirmed that he was a Reaper. He hadn't denied or agreed with her statement, but he didn't need to. "I saw something amazing and terrifying a few weeks ago. I don't know what happened, but I'm glad you were there. All of you. Thank you, because I'm not sure the Light could have handled the beasts alone."

"Trackers," he said. "They're called Trackers, and they were created by Usaeil."

Kyra glanced away, nodding slowly. "Is that why Usaeil was killed?"

"Were you at the castle when the battle between Usaeil and Rhi happened?" he asked instead of answering.

"No. I was looking for you, but it is all any Fae can talk about. Balladyn killed by Usaeil, and Usaeil taken down by Rhi. I think there's a bigger picture here that few people can see, though."

His silence was answer enough.

Kyra shifted, uncomfortable in the stillness of the forest. She didn't try to get away, even though it would probably be the right thing to do. But she liked talking to Dubhan, and she wanted to know more.

"What does this mean for me?" she finally asked.

He blew out a harsh breath. "You were in the wrong place at the wrong time."

"Was I?" she asked. "I don't think so. I got to see something no one else did. That happened for a reason."

Dubhan squeezed the bridge of his nose with his thumb and forefinger. "Kyra, you shouldn't have found me, and you really shouldn't have followed me."

"Is that one of the rules?"

His arm dropped to his side. "How did you find me?"

"I told you. I kept thinking about you while I was driving around on my motorbike. Next thing I knew, I arrived here and saw you."

"That's it? No spells, no magic?"

"Blood is needed to find someone. I don't use blood magic," she said, offended that he would even suggest that. It didn't matter that he didn't know her. His mind had immediately gone to taboo magic.

He held up his hands briefly. "My apologies. It's just . . . you shouldn't have been able to locate me."

She told herself to keep quiet, and yet her lips parted, and she said, "I actually found you four different times. The last one was this morning."

He closed his eyes and sighed.

Apprehension filled her at the pained look on his face. She had just made her plight worse. She didn't know how she knew that, but she did. Was she going to disappear like her aunt? Maybe that's exactly what had happened to Eva.

That thought didn't help Kyra's anxiety. Her mind raced to think of something—anything—that could keep her from harm.

"I can't explain why I'm drawn to you," she admitted. "It's inexplicable, but it's the truth. I've tried to leave, I've attempted to forget you, but I can't."

"Fate." His eyes opened and met hers. His glamour was gone, and his dark red gaze held hers captive. "It's Fate."

"And what does that mean for me?"

"I honestly don't know."

CHAPTER

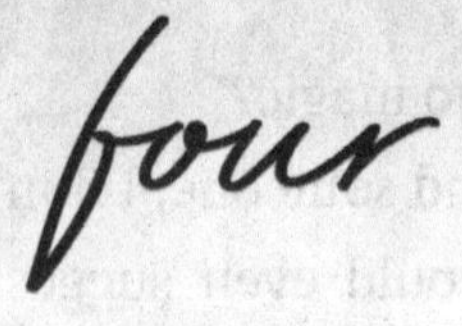

Dubhan had never been in this position before. He didn't know whether to contact Eoghan, his leader or even Death herself, to let them know what he'd learned about Kyra seeing him and the others at the Light Castle.

The fact that Kyra knew that he was a Reaper was enough to cause worry. It was the first rule of being a Reaper. No Fae could know who they were.

The rules weren't so cut and dried for a Halfling. Apparently, being part human helped in that situation. But Kyra was full Fae. Which led to other concerns. Some Fae knew who the Reapers were. Balladyn had, Rhi did, and so did Xaneth. Not to mention the Fae who were now lovers and wives of the current Reapers.

So, Dubhan honestly didn't know where the line was drawn anymore. It would most likely be Erith's decision, but he didn't want to call on Death yet. There was something about Kyra that made him instantly like her. And believe her.

She wasn't lying to him. Of that, he was sure. He would stake his very life on it. That in and of itself brought another question. He didn't know Kyra, so why was he willing to bet on her?

He didn't have an answer, and yet he was prepared to do just that.

"Dubhan?"

He loved the sound of his name on her lips. Dubhan inwardly shook himself and focused on the problem. Kyra looked at him with large, bright blue eyes. They weren't her natural color, nor was the pink hair hers. He wanted to see her for who she really was, not what glamour she chose to use that day.

But he didn't ask her to show him.

"You don't know what to do with me, do you?" she asked.

Her lips were turned up in a rueful smile as if she'd accepted her fate. And, somehow, that pissed him off.

"There has only ever been one other that I know of who could track one of us." He didn't say "Reapers," because he didn't want to confirm anything, although his admission was just that if anyone looked hard enough.

Kyra's interest appeared piqued. "Can you tell me who?"

Dubhan shook his head. "The thing is, no one should be able to."

"How did the other person do it?" she asked.

"I don't know for sure." It was something he would have to ask Cael the next time he saw him. No one had expected anyone other than Rhi to be able to pull off such a feat, and yet, here Kyra stood.

She licked her lips and eyed him. "Would it help if I tried to find out how I did it?"

Dubhan shook his head. "It's enough that you've done it. No need to do it again."

"It's not all of you," she said. "Just you."

He wasn't sure how to react to her statement. On the one hand, her admission made him happy for reasons he couldn't quite determine. On the other, he knew that no good could come of any of this.

Perhaps he needed to approach this another way. "You wanted to get to know me. Why?"

"You're a Reaper."

As if that said it all. Dubhan drew in a deep breath. "Did you have questions? Things you wanted to say?"

"I'm right, aren't I? You are a Reaper."

He tried to think of a way to answer her without actually answering her, but unfortunately, there wasn't such a reply.

"Why can't I know?" she asked. "I won't tell anyone."

Dubhan ran a hand down his face. Give him a battle facing hundreds of his enemies, and he could handle it. Give him a female with questions he couldn't answer, and he was out of his depth.

"I see," she said, her face crestfallen.

"Kyra," he said and briefly closed his eyes. "You weren't supposed to see anything at the Light Castle."

She cocked a brow. "Maybe not, but I did."

"Be that as it may, it doesn't change the fact that you can't keep following me."

"You're looking for something or someone, though. Maybe I can help."

He shook his head. "You can't. The best thing for you to do is to get far away from me and forget we ever spoke."

"I can't."

Those two words were all it took to seal her fate.

He hung his head. "Kyra, please."

She took a step closer. "I may not know much about Reapers,

but I've seen you, Dubhan. I've watched you for days. You're a good man. You're kind."

"I'm not remotely kind," he said as he lifted his head. "I'm far, far from that. And for all you know, the man I've shown you these past few days could be nothing more than an act to draw you out."

She seemed to think about that for a moment and shrugged. "It could have been, and if that's the case, then you fooled me. But it doesn't change the fact that I still want to know you."

"Why?"

"Because you're a Reaper," she said with a smile. "You're one who is feared and respected above all but Death. Fae actually tremble when the Reapers are mentioned."

He fisted his hands, not liking where this conversation was going. "And you want to use me now that you think you know who I am?"

She jerked back as if struck, her face scrunched in a frown. "No. Never."

"That's the only reason you could want to know me."

"There are other reasons. Like the fact that I think you're amazing. I know what I saw. All of you can do some serious damage in battle, but you"—she paused, smiling—"you, Dubhan, are exceptional. I've never seen anyone move like you do."

He didn't like how her praise made him want to stand up straighter. "And you've seen many battles?"

The smile died on her lips. "I've seen a couple, yes. And before you ask, I'm not a warrior. I have a few moves if I'm attacked, but my skills lay elsewhere."

"What skills are those?"

Her face suddenly split into a smile. "I'm really good with magic. I know spells most Fae don't."

"How is that?"

"My aunt had a spell book that came from the Fae Realm. It's incredibly old."

Now, he was intrigued. Spells like that weren't easy to come by. "Where did she get it?"

"She returned to the Fae Realm to retrieve some family things and went looking around. She said she found it in the rubble."

Dubhan wasn't so sure about how her aunt had found the book, but he'd question her more about that later. Perhaps he'd even have a talk with her aunt to find out who the book really belonged to. "Did you use one of those spells to find me?"

Kyra rolled her eyes. "I told you that I didn't."

"No, you said you just thought of me."

"Exactly. I'm not lying."

"I have no reason to believe you."

She crossed her arms over her chest. "You have no reason not to believe me."

"Actually, I've several." The minute the words were out of his mouth, he wanted to take them back—even though they were the truth.

Kyra dropped her arms and took a step back. "I see this is getting us nowhere. You don't believe me, and I have no way to prove anything to you. So, call whoever you need to."

"What?" he asked, confused.

"I get the idea that you don't want to deal with me. Which means, you'll be letting someone else know about me and what I've seen."

He wanted to tell her that she was wrong, but the words wouldn't come. Instead, he asked, "Have you noticed anything different about the village?"

"Drumshanbo? I wasn't really looking at the town. Did you find something? Is that why you've remained?"

He glanced around the forest and blew out a breath. "I'm looking for someone, but there is something about the village that has kept me here. I did find something."

"What?"

"A building. It's a bookstore run by a mortal."

Kyra shrugged, her lips twisting. "Nothing out of the ordinary there."

"Except there are two markings on the doorway. One is to keep Fae out."

"And the other?" she asked when he paused.

"It's a symbol I've seen one other time in my life. I don't know what it means, and I'd like to find out."

Kyra's brow furrowed as she stared at him. "Can't you ask the other Reapers?"

"I'd like to keep this to myself for now." Dubhan was aware that every time he answered in such a way, he was confirming without actually stating it that he was a Reaper.

"Show me," she urged him, holding out her hand.

Dubhan didn't immediately reach for her. He had brought it up to change the subject, but as soon as he did, a part of him hoped that she might know what the symbol was.

"I won't bite," she said, straight-faced. Then she grinned wickedly. "Much."

He couldn't stop the smile that pulled at his lips. He grasped her hand and took them to the alley across from the bookstore in Drumshanbo.

"Oh, I've seen this place," Kyra said as she studied the building. "You've walked past this several times."

"Yeah. I couldn't figure out why until recently."

She stared up at him. "I'd be happy to go look at it if you'd release me."

"The thing is, you shouldn't just walk up there."

Her gaze darted to the store before returning to him. "Why?"

"I don't know. A feeling."

"Was magic used?"

"Other than the symbol to keep Fae out? I don't think so."

She nodded and looked back at the building for a quiet moment. Then she faced him. "I can veil myself long enough to rush up there and get a look at things."

Fek. Dubhan couldn't believe he was going to do this, but he laced his fingers with hers. This could go wrong, so very wrong. But not even that thought could stop him from veiling them both. "Don't let go of me," he told her.

Then he started walking.

Halfway across the street, she gaped at him. "We're veiled, aren't we? You can hold a veil this long? Not just for you, but for another, as well? That's incredible."

Again, he didn't answer. What could he say?

"I won't tell anyone," she replied in a much more sedate tone.

They made it to the bookstore's door, and she grew quiet. They both studied the symbols for several tense moments, then she gave him a nod. They turned as one and retraced their steps. It wasn't until they were back in the alley and out of sight that he released her.

The moment their hands disconnected, he wanted to reach for her again. It was almost like he'd found some sort of comfort holding onto her, and having her hold onto him. It was . . . odd. And very enjoyable.

And something he wasn't interested in delving deeper into. Kyra was beautiful, and he was attracted to her. That was enough for him to send her away. The fact that he was feeling . . . things . . . didn't bode well.

At all.

"I've never seen that marking before," Kyra told him.

Damn. He'd really hoped she might know what it was because returning to his family to get answers wasn't an option. "Thanks for looking."

"I said I didn't know. That doesn't mean I can't ask around or even do some research myself." She suddenly frowned. "Come to think of it, there is something that might help. Come," she said.

No sooner did the word fall from her lips than she grabbed his hand and teleported them. Dubhan found himself inside her cottage. She released him and made a beeline for the coffee table where a large book rested.

She sat and patted the sofa next to her. "This is the spell book I told you about. There's a section in here that I skimmed through but didn't really read. It has symbols that could be used by the humans against us."

He made his way to her and sat on the edge of the cushion. "Who told the humans how to stand against us?"

"I don't know," Kyra said with a shrug as she flipped through the book. Finally, she found the page and pointed. "There."

Sure enough, there were well over four dozen different symbols that could do all manner of things to Fae, from keeping them from entering a building, to removing their glamour.

"I've only ever seen the one to keep the Fae out," he said.

"Uh, hm. And I don't see your other symbol here. Odd that the humans would forget all these other markings."

He looked through the list again, hoping he might have overlooked what he was searching for, but it wasn't there.

"Where else have you seen the symbol?" she asked.

Dubhan turned his head to her and said, "On the door of my parents' home."

CHAPTER

Dubhan's admission rocked Kyra. "Your parents?"

He gave a slight nod of his head as if he didn't want to admit it a second time.

"They never told you what it was?"

His red gaze slid away from her. She liked that he hadn't used glamour again. There was something about gazing into his crimson orbs that hypnotized her.

"Asking questions wasn't done in that house."

She noted that he didn't say "my home" or even "my house." It was the house. And that was very telling. She almost asked him what type of childhood he'd had, but if he didn't want to discuss a symbol, he certainly wasn't going to tell her about his past.

And since she hadn't brought up her family, she wasn't going to push.

"How did you learn anything if you couldn't ask questions?" she asked.

Dubhan shrugged and got to his feet. He walked a few paces before he turned to look at her. "My father's philosophy was that he showed us what needed to be done, and we followed suit. We didn't ask why or how. We simply did it."

We. That meant Dubhan had at least one other sibling. They had that in common, at least. His words, however, spoke volumes, but maybe that was because she was listening harder than most others would.

Kyra quietly closed the book and folded her hands in her lap. "I can't imagine that was an easy way to grow up."

"There was nothing about my life that was easy."

His gaze slid away, which firmly shut the door on his past. Kyra didn't dare ask more about it, no matter how desperately she wanted to know. It wasn't as if she could heal his wounds, mainly because there were none. There were only scars.

And they went soul-deep.

"There are a couple of people I can ask about the marking," she told him. "They might not know anything, but it's the only place I know to start if you don't want to ask your friends or family."

Red eyes cut back to her. "You would do that for me?"

"Why not?" she asked with a shrug. "It's not like I'm doing anything grand or noble. I'm just asking some people a question."

A muscle ticked in his jaw. "My instinct tells me that whatever the symbol is, you need to tread carefully."

"I always do."

"Kyra," he began, then stopped. After a moment, he said, "I'm not sure you should ask about it."

She got to her feet. "I may not be a warrior, but I know how to take care of myself. Besides, something has continued to draw you to that bookstore. You were meant to find that symbol, and you need to know what it is."

"I don't need to know. I want to know."

She rolled her eyes. "Trust me, you need to know. Otherwise, it wouldn't be digging at you like a bird pecking at an insect."

For a fraction of an instant, his lips tipped into a grin. "You do have a way with words."

"It doesn't matter what I say around my mother, she's always offended by it. I'm not the daughter she wanted, but I am who I am."

His head leaned to the side. "Why isn't she happy with who you are?"

"Because I'm not the lady she, my sister, or all the other women of the family are. I don't want to wear heels and dresses and spend time at court, looking for a husband. I would rather be in my boots, riding my motorbike around, doing whatever makes me happy."

Dubhan blinked. "And you did what you wanted?"

She laughed, thinking back to that difficult time. "I did, because I knew it was my life, and I had to be the one to live it, not my mother or anyone else. It put a huge rift between my family and me. My aunt, Eva, who had been through the same thing as me, stepped in and helped me find a path that made me happy but didn't alienate me from the family."

"The same aunt who found the spell book?"

"Yes. She didn't want me to make the same mistakes she did. After she'd made her choice, she never spoke to anyone in the family again. I knew about her because she found me when I was just a child. I saw her every few centuries or so. It wasn't until I was forging my own path that she told me she had seen the same qualities in me that she'd discovered in herself and wanted to help."

Dubhan's eyes widened for a moment. "And you took her help?"

"I didn't see how it could hurt. Besides, I didn't want to lose my family. I wanted them to accept me for who I was, just as I accepted them for who they were. I didn't want to be forced to change or conform to their standards."

He made a sound in the back of his throat. "That never occurred to me. My path was laid out, and I followed it."

"There's nothing wrong with that, either. Everyone has a path. Besides, had you not taken that road, you wouldn't be where you are now. I try to think of all the mistakes I made—and will make —as learning experiences. I must need those events to happen in order for them to help me out with something in the future. You had to walk your path because you were meant to be a Reaper. That's your true path. Not your past."

"Maybe," he murmured.

Kyra glanced at the spell book. "Let me go ask about the symbol while you continue doing whatever it is you're doing."

"I'd feel better if I went with you."

Was he worried about her? That made her stomach flutter in excitement. "I'll be fine."

"I can go veiled. No one but you will know I'm there."

"I've forged these relationships on trust. I won't lie to them now."

Dubhan gave a nod of acceptance. "I respect that, but you should always expect that someone will betray you."

"That's a horrible way to live."

"It's the only way to live."

"Is that what happened to you? Were you betrayed?"

"Yes."

One word. That was all she was going to get. And, frankly, she was surprised she'd gotten that much. "I'm sorry."

"I'm not. I hated my life then. As you said, I'm meant to be here."

"I'm still sorry you were betrayed."

"No matter what people say, you should always expect the worst."

Kyra shook her head slowly. "People lie, cheat, steal, and kill. Those are facts. I know it's going to happen to someone, and possibly to me. But I'd rather live my life looking at the beauty of things and finding peace within myself rather than holding onto negativity."

"Being smart isn't negative. You can still be happy and have peace while also being smart and aware of how people are."

Obviously, they were going to have to agree to disagree. "I won't be long. Where do I find you?"

"Just call my name. I'll find you."

She gave him a smile and then teleported to Belfast and a small store hidden in the depths of the city. She ignored the other Fae around her and walked straight to the door of the herbal shop that sold herbs but also magic if you knew what to ask for. She entered, a bell clinking overhead as she did. Her gaze instantly moved to the right where a counter stood, and behind it, a couple.

"Tate. Jesta. How are things?" she asked.

The elderly couple was Light Fae who used glamour to age themselves from young to old through the years so the mortals wouldn't realize who and what they were. This was the fifth time the couple had reached their mid-seventies. It wouldn't be long before they died, the store passing down to another family member—aka Tate and Jesta—and they started all over again.

"It's been a while, Kyra," Jesta said, her gray eyes going sharp.

Kyra nodded. "It has."

Tate grinned. "You still have the motorbike?"

"Of course," Kyra answered. "I've been riding around and seeing the world. You two should buy one and travel. It's amazing to feel the wind flying by you."

"Been traveling for work?" Tate asked as he fidgeted.

Kyra didn't say anything about Tate's nervousness as she shrugged and shot a smile at Jesta, who hadn't said anything else. "I've not really been doing much work lately. Taking some time off from trading secrets between the Dark and Light."

Jesta didn't return the grin. The usually friendly Fae looked as if she had swallowed a lemon. "It's good to see you."

"Somehow, I don't believe you. What's going on?" Kyra stated. She was used to looking for signs that someone was lying to her. She had to be on her toes when she dealt with the Dark and even the Light, as well as the humans.

"Nothing," Tate said hurriedly.

Kyra looked from Tate to Jesta. "You might as well tell me. I'll find out eventually."

It was Jesta who let out a loud sigh. "Your mother was here."

Her mother? Here? What the hell was that about? Kyra put her hands on the counter, a frown forming. "What did she say?"

"That we would be wise to no longer deal with you."

Tate nodded. "She also said she would be reporting us to the next person who takes the Light throne."

Kyra couldn't believe what she was hearing. "First, my mother is crazy. Don't listen to her. Second, I'm sorry you had to deal with her. Third, who cares who she tells about you? You run a business like many other Fae who cater to both our kind and humans."

Tate and Jesta exchanged a look, neither willing to meet Kyra's gaze.

Kyra winced. "You never registered your business with the throne, did you?"

"We rectified that," Tate said.

Jesta nodded quickly. "But we were fined heavily for waiting as long as we did."

"Well, it's done, and no one can hold that over your head now."

Tate shrugged. "True. But these are our problems. You don't need to worry about that. What can we do for you?"

"Tate," Jesta admonished as she snapped her head in his direction.

He put his hand on top of Jesta's. "We don't mess in family affairs, but Kyra is a grown woman. She's always been honest and fair to us in the past."

Jesta sighed and gave Kyra an apologetic look. "He does make a fine point. You're one of the few we can befriend. And you send the best mortals to us for business. Tell us what you need."

"What I'm usually here for. Information." Kyra used her finger, pushing magic through the tip to trace the symbol on the counter in pink to match her hair. "Have either of you ever seen this before?"

The couple studied the marking for several moments before they shook their heads.

"Sorry," Tate said with a frown.

Kyra forced a smile she didn't feel. "Thanks. Do you know who might be able to give me an answer?"

"Maximillian," Jesta said.

Tate glanced at his wife and nodded. He always seems to know about obscure things like this. What is it, though?"

"It was found along with a symbol to keep Fae out," Kyra explained.

Jesta's brows drew together. "On a mortal's door?"

"Yeah."

"When you find out what it is, can you let us know?" Jesta asked worriedly.

Kyra flashed them a bright smile. "Consider it done. And, next time, just don't let my mother or anyone from my family inside. Trust me, you'll be better off."

She waved to the couple and walked from the building, happy that she had someone who might give her what she needed. Once out on the sidewalk, she paused and looked one way and then the other. Kyra knew of Maximillian and where to find him. A Fae in her line of work had to know where to go for the impossible. However, she knew him better than most. He almost always had whatever answer someone sought, his price was steep.

Too steep.

However, she wouldn't know what the price would be until she met with him. For all she knew, he'd want something she could easily give him.

She had considered going to him about Eva, but in the end, Kyra had thought better of it. There had been something in her gut that told her he should be her last resort. The fact that she willingly followed a Reaper instead of going to a Fae spoke volumes about how dangerous Maximillian could be.

Kyra teleported to Dublin and made her way through the streets until she came to a dilapidated building with a NO TRESPASSING sign with CONDEMNED right below it. She looked around to make sure no one was watching, then veiled herself for as long as it took to enter the building. She ascended the stairs to the third floor and started down the hallway. At the third door on the left, she stopped and faced it.

To a human, it appeared as nothing more than a door with chipped paint and rusty hinges. To a Fae, it was a doorway straight to Maximillian and wherever his current hiding place was.

She took a deep breath and turned the handle. The door opened, and without hesitation, she stepped over the threshold and into the tiny hovel where the reclusive—and slightly mad—Light Fae lived.

CHAPTER
six

It took Dubhan all of ten seconds to decide to follow Kyra. It wasn't because he didn't trust her, but that there was a nagging thought in the back of his head that the symbol was dangerous.

Dangerous enough to cause him worry, which meant it wasn't something just any Fae should look into.

He had no trouble tracking Kyra to Belfast, and he was impressed by the way she'd handled a situation that could've gone very badly with the Fae couple. But when they mentioned Maximillian, Dubhan immediately tensed.

His first reaction was to reach for Kyra and make sure she couldn't get to the recluse, but he stopped himself. He didn't want her to know that he was with her because he was only there in case she got into trouble. And now that he knew she was headed to Maximillian's, he was doubly glad he'd tagged along.

Though he suspected she wasn't going to be happy about it at all.

When he went to walk through the Fae doorway, he hesitated. Some inner voice told him that if he went through, things wouldn't go smoothly. But it was that same worry about Kyra that made him ignore that voice and follow her anyway.

The moment he stepped through, it felt as if a thousand blades pierced him. Dubhan held back his bellow and steeled himself against the onslaught. His gaze found Kyra, and he saw her walking through with no problem. That meant whatever was happening to him had something to do with the fact that he was a Reaper.

Dubhan was about to give up and go back through the doorway when he spotted Max looking young, vibrant, and happy. All the old anger and hurt rose up, spewing within Dubhan like a volcano erupting. If he hadn't been in such pain, he would've attacked the bastard.

Maximillian's hair was cut short and slicked back while his silver eyes locked on Kyra from where he sat on his chair before a roaring fire. He said nothing, simply stared at her. Dubhan couldn't tell if the two knew each other or not. He wasn't sure if it would be better if Kyra didn't know Max or if she did. Regardless, the sooner Kyra was away from the Light, the better.

"I didn't think I'd ever see you again," Maximillian said.

Dubhan inwardly cringed.

Kyra didn't move from her spot. "Hi, Max."

"No explanation as to why you didn't come back before now?" he asked.

Dubhan narrowed his gaze on Max. The bastard now had a smile on his face as if he were happy to see Kyra. And Dubhan certainly didn't like the way Max was eyeing Kyra.

"I told you, our time was up," Kyra said. "It was nice while our affair lasted, but I needed to move on."

Dubhan's mouth fell open. He looked between them, unable to believe that the two had been lovers.

Max sat back, displaying a simple white shirt and dark jeans. He might live in a small place, but everything in it served a purpose. At one time, Dubhan had actually looked up to Max. He had shunned everything unimportant and lived as simply as a Fae could. Max sustained himself by learning everything he could—and selling it for a price.

"I cared for you," Max told Kyra. "Deeply."

Kyra kept her voice neutral. "And I care for you. Still."

"But you aren't with me."

"No," she said with a shake of her head. "I'm not. And you know why."

Max rose swiftly and closed the distance between him and Kyra. "We were good together. We could be again."

"I'm sorry, Max. No." She stated it firmly, moving back to keep space between them.

His face fell into a deep frown. "Isn't that why you returned?"

"Actually, I'm here because I need something."

Max stepped back as if he were putting a wall around himself. "I see."

Dubhan closed his eyes as pain throbbed through him. He didn't know how much longer he'd be able to stand the agony, but he couldn't leave Kyra. Max was the worst kind of Fae. He took advantage of others while also manipulating them.

"There is a symbol I've come across that I can't find anything about," Kyra explained.

Max nodded shrewdly. "And you think I can help."

"You probably can. It'll depend on what your price for the information is, however."

Max laughed and resumed his seat. "You haven't changed at

all, Kyra. Still looking for the best deal without giving too much. What does the symbol look like?"

This time, Kyra used her magic to draw it in the air. Dubhan kept his gaze on Max, squinting as the throbbing intensified and caused his vision to blur at the edges. Despite the pain, Dubhan saw Max's eyes widen slightly before he wiped all emotion from his face. The fekker knew something. The question was whether Max would tell Kyra the truth or not.

That was another thing most people didn't realize—Max lied. A lot. Half the time, he didn't know the answers, but he knew just enough to make people believe he did. Max felt no remorse for lying and taking whatever someone was willing to pay for information.

"Where did you see that symbol?" Max demanded.

Kyra stared at him. "I can't remember."

"You know exactly where. Tell me."

"Tell me what it is."

Max clenched his jaw. "Kyra, I don't know what you're mixed up in, but whatever it is, forget it. Stop asking questions, and don't go back to the place you saw the marking."

Dubhan forgot the pain as he watched Max. Something was definitely up with the Fae, and he really wished he could question Max himself. But that wasn't possible—and not simply because Dubhan was veiled.

"What do you know, Max?" Kyra pressed as she took a step toward him.

Max's head jerked to her. "Did you not hear what I said? This is serious."

"Tell me what it is that's frightened you."

Max gave a bark of laughter. "By the stars, you're stubborn. I'm not telling you any more than you already know."

"You're just saying this to hike up the price. You forget, I've seen you do this to others. I know your methods."

In a blink, Max was on his feet and standing within inches of Kyra. Dubhan moved beside her, ready to lash out at Max, regardless of how much pain he was in. It was all Dubhan could do to stay on his feet, but he would be there to get Kyra away from Max.

"Kyra, stop. Stop all of it," Max demanded, his face stony with anger and apprehension. "If you don't want to die, you'll leave all of this alone. I'm not playing here. I'm not trying to get anything. What I am trying to do is warn you."

She rolled her eyes. "What's your price?" When he didn't answer, she crossed her arms over her chest and cocked her hip. "You always have a price. Give it to me."

For several minutes, Max didn't utter a word. His gaze narrowed as he composed himself. "My price is that you stay here with me and never ask about any of this again."

Dubhan blinked, unsure if he'd heard Max correctly with the ringing in his head.

"What?" Kyra asked with a choked laugh. "That's not going to happen."

Max gave her a nod, his lips compressing. "That's my price."

She sighed loudly and rolled her eyes. "I really thought you would work with me. I didn't come thinking you'd give me something for free, but I didn't think you'd try to work me like you do with others."

"I'm not."

He seemed sincere, though Dubhan wished it were otherwise. Dubhan couldn't tell Kyra that, however. He looked at her to find her defiant and ready to stay as long as it took to get what she wanted.

Max suddenly frowned and stepped back as he looked around. "Who did you bring?"

Kyra made a face. "Bring? I didn't bring anyone."

"There's someone here."

"Max, you know as well as I do that no Fae can remain veiled for that long. I'm by myself."

Dubhan watched Kyra's face. She said all the right words, but he saw the tightness in her lips. She had figured out that he was here, and she wasn't happy about it. At least, she hadn't given him up.

Yet.

Max leaned close to Kyra and whispered, "I know you. You get something in your head, and you don't stop until you're satisfied."

"I'm tenacious."

"You're fekking stubborn. And this time, it could cost you your life," he said tightly, his face mottled with anger.

Kyra laughed, but it wasn't so relaxed this time. "Why do you say that?"

His nostrils flared as he shook his head. "There are some things even I don't mess with. I think you're somehow involved with both."

"Both?" Kyra asked, her brows drawing together.

Dubhan wanted her to push Max and find out what he'd meant by that, but Max turned his back on her, his hand slashing through the air. "You should leave. Don't ask anyone else about that symbol."

"Whatever." Kyra had already turned around to walk back to the doorway.

"Wait!" Max yelled and moved to stand in front of her. "Have you gone to anyone else about the marking?"

Kyra vacillated. After a moment, she gave a nod. "One other place."

Dubhan grimaced and bit his tongue, trying not to cry out in pain. He needed to listen because he was beginning to suspect that Max might be telling the truth.

"You shouldn't have done that. What did they tell you?" Max demanded.

Kyra shrugged and said, "They told me to see you."

Max raked a hand through his short, black hair as he paced in agitation. "Fek. This is bad."

Dubhan realized they needed to leave. And soon. But he couldn't go without Kyra.

He wouldn't go without her.

By now, Kyra was frowning. It was obvious that even she was beginning to believe Max. "It's just a symbol."

"It's so much more than that," Max said. He stopped and looked at Kyra. "You really have stepped into something you shouldn't have, darling."

"I need to be prepared, then."

Max sighed loudly and nodded. "Unfortunately, you're right, but once I give you this knowledge, you'll be hunted."

"You have the answers I seek," Kyra said angrily. "I knew you did."

Max snorted loudly. Acid dripped from his voice as he spoke. "Do you really think I live like this, hidden away, never going out because I want to? Think again, darling."

"But anyone can find you if they want to."

"Not the ones I'm hiding from. Why do you think the doorway here is covered in hidden markings?"

Now, Dubhan knew why he was in so much pain. Damn, he should've looked. He turned his head to glance at the doorway and found numerous symbols there, some of them running together. Or was that just the pain affecting his eyesight? Shite. He really didn't know.

But he was aware that he was losing strength and quickly. If he didn't get out soon, he would collapse, and he wasn't sure if the veil would stay up if he did.

"What kind of symbols?" Kyra asked.

Dubhan bent over, drawing in deep breaths of air to try and keep most of the pain manageable. He stared at the rug beneath his feet while he listened to them.

"Everything," Max said with a shrug.

She gave him a pointed look. "Give me an example."

"I've made sure that Usaeil can't find me, and if she can't find me, then neither can her Trackers. I've also ensured that my soul can't be taken by Reapers."

Dubhan was barely hanging on now, but even hearing that, he wanted to snort. The pain was excruciating as it radiated through his entire body, ringing like a bell.

"Reapers?" Kyra asked softly.

Max nodded. "Believe in them, Kyra. They're real."

"How do you know?"

"I've made it my business to know all sorts of things."

Dubhan raised his head and speared Max with a look of hatred. Max just thought he could keep away from Reapers. Dubhan wanted to drop the veil and prove that the symbols would do nothing to protect Max from Reapers or Death. Then Kyra spoke, reminding Dubhan what he was really there for.

She swallowed. "What is the symbol I asked you about?"

Max walked past her and took his seat, leaning forward so that his elbows rested on his knees. His face was turned toward the fire, bathing his skin in red-orange light. "A very long time ago, Druids from another realm came here. They were strong, but they couldn't defeat the Dragon Kings."

Dubhan forced himself to listen at the mention of the Dragon Kings because this was information the Reapers, Death, and the Kings needed to know. But the pain was eating him from the inside out.

"The Druids brought mortals without magic here, and the Kings made a place for them without realizing that there was an ulterior motive."

Kyra's mouth fell open. "You're joking."

"No," Max said, still not looking at her. "The Druids waited until some of the mortals developed magic, and while that was happening, they went to the Fae and found allies among our kind. Light and Dark Fae were brought together, along with good and bad Druids of Earth. The three separate entities joined their magic together in an effort to take down the Dragon Kings. They call themselves the Others. And there are always those looking to join the ranks."

Kyra was quiet, simply staring at Max. Dubhan felt sick to his stomach because he had a suspicion about where the story was going.

Lights sparked in Dubhan's eyes. He knew he couldn't last much longer. He was holding on by a thread that was slipping through his fingers.

Max took a deep breath before he said, "Anyone with that symbol marked anywhere has declared themselves with the Others." Max turned his head to Kyra. "And they will take down anyone who stands in their way."

CHAPTER
seven

Kyra was shaken to her core. Even after she'd left Max's, she couldn't stop hearing his final words as she stood in the dilapidated building. She looked around, waiting for Dubhan to show himself. She wasn't angry that he had followed her. She was irritated.

She had no reason to be mad since he didn't know her and had no cause to trust her. But as the minutes ticked by, and she didn't see him, she began to worry. Maybe it hadn't been him with her at Max's.

"Dubhan."

His name echoed through the abandoned halls, bouncing off doors before fading away. Still, he didn't materialize. She turned and looked at the doorway to Maximillian's. He'd said he put up wards to keep Reapers out. If that was true, Dubhan wouldn't have been able to get through. Would he? She honestly didn't know, because he seemed like the type who wouldn't let anything stand in his way if he wanted something.

She turned back around and jumped when she spotted Dubhan leaning against the door opposite her, looking ill. His breathing was ragged, and his face was pale. His eyes were closed as if it were a struggle to remain on his feet.

"It was you with me," she said.

His red eyes briefly opened to meet hers. "I was worried . . . something might . . . happen to you."

The fact that he had difficulty talking told her just what that symbol had done to him. She walked to him and put her arm around his waist as she slung his arm over her shoulders. But he didn't pull away from the door.

"Let me help you," she said when he resisted.

"I can do this."

She rolled her eyes. "You're about to fall on your face. Should I release you so you can?"

"You're sassy," he muttered.

That made her smile because Eva had often told her that. "I sure am. Now, come on. It's not weakness to let someone take care of you."

With a loud sigh, he leaned his full weight on her. Kyra wasn't prepared for it, and her knees nearly buckled. She managed to stay on her feet and teleport them back to her cottage right next to the sofa just in time for him to tip sideways. Kyra shifted so Dubhan fell on the cushions, but she ended up going down with him.

It wasn't until she slid off the edge of the couch that she realized he had passed out. She got to her knees and gently moved his heavy arm from around her shoulders. He was half on his side, half on his stomach. With barely a thought, she used magic to turn him onto his back so he rested more comfortably.

Kyra then took that time to return to Belfast to warn Jesta and Tate. She studied the shop first for any signs of danger, but everything appeared normal. It wasn't until she walked in and found the shop empty that she began to worry.

She called out to the couple, but her query was met with silence. Kyra made her way around the counter to the back of the shop, but she found nothing out of place, and no sign of either Tate or Jesta. She turned and took a step, her foot sinking into something. When she looked down, she saw two piles of ash.

Kyra jumped back, her heart pounding in fear and shock as she gazed at what was left of the couple. She glanced around to make sure no one else was in the shop before hurriedly teleporting to her cottage. Her hands shook uncontrollably as she put up more wards around her home, but she wasn't sure that would keep the Others out.

"What happened?"

She whirled around at the sound of Dubhan's voice. She was so glad he was here. She didn't want to be alone. Not now.

"Kyra," he pressed as he sat up, a worried frown creasing his brow.

"Tate and Jesta. They're . . . dead."

Remorse came over his face. "I'm sorry."

"Is it because of the questions I asked? Did I do this to them like Max said?"

Dubhan rose to his feet and went to her. He was steadier now, but he still looked a bit green around the gills. "This isn't your fault. It's mine."

"I'm the one who talked to them."

He took her hands in his. "This is on me. It's all on me. I never should've asked you about it."

She shook her head and moved closer to him, needing his warmth. Talking about the couple was too difficult right now. She needed to think of something else. "How were you able to go to Max's if he used the symbol to keep out Reapers?"

"It wasn't easy," he confessed. "It hurt like hell."

"I can tell. You look better now."

"I'd like to know how he found the Reaper symbol to keep us out. I've never heard of it before."

She enjoyed that they were still touching, and she wondered if he realized it. It wasn't like she was going to release him. She had dreamed of him touching her for so long, she wasn't going to pass up the opportunity to experience it for real. And he felt so very good.

Her thoughts returned to the issue at hand. "There's much Max knows that he isn't telling."

"You can't believe everything he says."

Kyra cocked her head to the side when she heard the note of anger in Dubhan's voice. "You know Max?"

"I did at one time."

She studied Dubhan. He'd said the words off-handedly, but it was obvious that he was trying to hide something. His anger was too palpable to be ignored. "What did he do?" Because Max had obviously done something.

"It doesn't matter. Just don't trust everything he says as truth."

She tightened her fingers on Dubhan's. "I know what kind of person Max is. He can be kind, but he looks out for himself first and foremost."

"You two were lovers."

She'd been prepared for this from the moment she realized that Dubhan had followed her. It had been a very long time since she'd talked about Max or even thought about him. "For a time. I was just starting out, moving between the Light and Dark, learning secrets, and trading them as well as items. We were only together a few months, but I saw who he really was during that time, and I didn't like it. That's when I ended things between us."

Dubhan held her gaze, looking deep into her eyes. Kyra wondered what he saw there, or maybe he was searching for something. She was an open book. There wasn't anything in her life that she kept secret. If someone wanted to know something, all they had to do was ask.

"Do you still care for him?" Dubhan asked.

Kyra shrugged. "We ended things amicably, at least we did to my way of thinking. I hold no animosity toward him. But I wouldn't consider Max a friend if that's what you're asking."

"Good to know."

"What did he do to you?"

"Let's just say I hold a great deal of animosity toward him."

"Oh." Kyra hated that Max had hurt Dubhan, and she really wanted to know the cause of it.

"It's a story for another day."

"I'm sorry."

"You have nothing to apologize for."

She gave him a weak smile. "I feel like I do, simply because of my association with Max."

"No," Dubhan said in a soft voice, his crimson eyes looking into hers.

His thumb rubbed the back of one of her hands. She liked the way it felt, and she relished having this connection with him.

Suddenly, Dubhan released her hands and took a step back. "Have you heard of the Others before?"

"No," Kyra said with a shake of her head. She struggled to find something to do with her hands now that they no longer held Dubhan's. "Have you?"

He nodded. "Unfortunately. They're nasty business."

"And they're after the Dragon Kings?"

"As a matter of fact, the Kings have been dealing with the Others for some time now. They'll need to know this new information. Especially the part about there being more who wish to join them. Up to this point, we all assumed their numbers were limited."

Dubhan sharing the information meant that he was leaving. Sadness filled Kyra at the thought. She wondered if she'd see him again, but she couldn't bring herself to pose the question for fear of what she might hear. "The Reapers need to know, as well."

"Yes," he admitted a heartbeat later.

Kyra wrapped her arms around herself, suddenly chilled. "You'll have to tell them about me."

He gave a single nod.

Kyra probably shouldn't worry about the Others right now. Her concern should be on the Reapers and what her knowledge of them meant for her. "I understand."

"Do you?" Dubhan asked with a quirked brow.

Instead of answering, she asked, "What about the person you've been looking for? Do you think they're here?"

Dubhan blew out a breath, his eyes moving over her shoulder to the window that looked out over the village from the mountain. "I'm beginning to think we'll never find him."

"Who is it? Maybe I can help."

Dubhan's crimson gaze slid back to her as he smiled. "You've already put your life in danger today. Why would you want to continue helping me?"

"To be around you," she answered honestly.

He blinked, apparently unprepared for her answer. "Why?"

"I like you."

"You don't know me."

She smiled sadly as she glanced away. "I've always had a habit of following my gut or heart or whatever leads me down one road or another. I've had some amazing adventures, seen stunning things, and have been a part of wonderful groups. Everything I've done, every decision I made, has been done by listening to this," she said and touched her chest. "I don't question it. I simply let it happen."

"You've been hurt."

Kyra shrugged, her lips twisting. "Everyone has. It's part of living. How can you expect to live, if you're worried about someone betraying you or having your heart broken? Yes, I've been hurt. I've been wronged, and I've had my heart broken. But they're experiences I don't regret. Nor would I trade them for anything."

"You wouldn't take away the pain?" Dubhan wore a small frown as if he couldn't comprehend what she was saying.

"No, because I learned something from it. I grew as a person, as well. Living is what I crave. I want to see the beauty in things, I want to experience as much as I can."

His lips softened as his expression smoothed. "That sounds nice."

"It is. You should try it."

"I will."

She smiled at him, her arms dropping to her sides. "That makes me happy to hear."

"Why me?" he asked.

Her gaze ran over him. "First, you're incredibly handsome. Watching you in battle . . . well, it was breathtaking. You are you. You don't use a mortal's interest in you to your advantage. In fact, you ignore them. No matter what you were in the past, you are something wonderful now."

"I was a Dark."

He said it as if it summed up everything. And she believed it did in a way, though she couldn't say why exactly. Wouldn't he always be a Dark? "You're a Reaper now."

"Don't make me out to be something I'm not. I did terrible things before."

She studied him for a moment, seeing him for who he really was—and still, she craved him with a hunger she knew would never be sated. "I know. Your past is right there in your red eyes and the silver in your hair."

"And . . . that doesn't bother you?"

In response, she walked to him, rose up on her toes, and pressed her mouth against his. For a heartbeat, he did nothing. Then his arms wrapped around her, and his head tilted to the side. His tongue slid along the seam of her lips, and she parted them for him. The first taste of his kiss was sublime, sending waves of pleasure through her until her body was on fire. She wound her arms around his neck and gave in to the wildly erotic hunger that swept through both of them.

He began to pull back. She gripped his face on either side of his head and said between kisses, "Don't you dare stop."

His hold on her tightened as he deepened the kiss. Desire pulsed through her, centering at her sex that throbbed with need. Kyra used magic to remove their clothes. Without missing a beat, Dubhan had her against a wall.

He went down on his knees and hooked one of her legs over his shoulder, then he pressed his lips against her sex. Kyra moaned as he licked and laved her clit. She threaded her fingers in his hair and gave in to the pleasure. The feel of his hands roaming over her hips, thighs, and butt lulled her while his tongue and mouth sent her spiraling into ecstasy.

When he pushed a finger inside her, Kyra gasped. The pleasure doubled, putting her on the edge of an orgasm quicker than she had ever been before. And just as quickly, he slowed his tongue.

She moaned in regret and rocked her hips, wanting more, but he didn't give it to her. That's when she realized that her body was his. Dubhan was the one in control of when she got her release. She didn't know when she had become his in that way. For all she knew, it was when she'd watched him battle the Trackers, but it didn't matter. She liked exactly where she was.

He kept her teetering on the edge, bringing her close to climax and then backing off. It made her insane with need until she was whispering his name over and over.

Then, finally, he pushed her over the edge.

The sound of her pleasure made him hard, aching to be inside her. Dubhan continued licking her until she sagged against the wall, the last of the orgasm leaving her weak and barely able to hold herself up.

He moved her leg from his shoulder and stood. Then he lifted her so her legs wrapped around his waist. Their eyes met, clashed. Her glamour fell away to reveal her pale silver orbs and shoulder-length, wavy, black hair.

Dubhan wasn't even sure she knew it had happened, but he liked it nonetheless. Seeing the real Kyra, stripped of not only her clothes, but her magic as well, made his heart catch.

She was stunning. Her body utter perfection, from her small breasts to the sexy indent of her waist. Her hands didn't stop touching him. Her fingers were soft, her caresses both gentle and erotic at the same time.

He held her, pinning her between his body and the wall. Her lips parted as her chest rose and fell quickly. A blush stained her skin from the exertion. She placed her palms on his chest, one hand over his heart. Then she undulated her hips as if seeking his arousal.

Dubhan ground his teeth together as a surge of hunger tore through him. He shifted so the head of his cock brushed against the swollen folds of her sex. Her breath hitched as their bodies made contact.

"I need to feel you inside me," she told him.

He rocked his hips forward, pushing the tip of his rod into her. Kyra bit her lip and tried to move, but he held her captive, refusing to allow her to do anything but feel what he was doing to her, absorbing the pleasure that swirled between them.

Dubhan pushed into her another inch. She leaned her head back against the wall, a moan falling from her lips. But when she realized that he wasn't going any deeper, she frowned, trying once more to shift so she could pull him in more. He grinned at her frustration, at the way her body sought his.

After a few moments, he shifted. Her hands moved to his shoulders, and her nails dug into his skin. She was whimpering now, her need that intense.

Gradually, he pushed more of his cock inside her, deeper and deeper. She was too intent on her own craving to realize how much the slowness of what they were doing affected him, as well. With one final push, he filled her completely. Then there was no stopping him.

He began rocking his hips, thrusting in an even rhythm. But soon, that wasn't enough. He pushed deeper, harder, flinging them both toward the precipice of pleasure as they kissed wildly. That's when he stopped moving.

Their breathing was heavy, their bodies slick with sweat. He turned and carried her to the bedroom. Their lips met for another fiery kiss as her hand roamed over his chest, back, and shoulders.

Dubhan sat on the mattress and kissed down her throat. He leaned her back over his arms as his lips trailed across her chest to her breasts. Her moan as he took a turgid peak into his mouth made his balls tighten.

She rocked her hips in time with the motion of his tongue, her soft cries filling the room. His mouth moved to her other nipple, where he teased that one mercilessly as he felt her body tightening for another climax.

He didn't relent, didn't slow as he pushed her over the edge. The feel of her body clamping around him as she orgasmed was electrifying.

When she sagged in his arms, he pulled out of her and moved her to her stomach with her legs hanging off the bed. He grasped her hips and entered her from behind with one push. Her gasp filled the silence of the room, followed quickly by his moan.

Her body still twitched from pleasure, pushing him to find his own. He rubbed his hands over her firm ass cheeks before he began moving in and out of her. With her dark hair covering half of her face as she lay on one cheek, she dug her fingers into the coverlet, moaning in ecstasy.

She rose up on her hands and pushed back, meeting him thrust for thrust. Then she looked over her shoulder at him, their gazes meeting. The desire he saw there pushed him past the point of rational thought. All he cared about, all that mattered was the bliss that awaited them.

And she would be coming with him when he climaxed.

He wanted to hear her scream once more, to see the way her body tensed and then shivered when the ecstasy took her. Dubhan reached around and found her clit, circling it with his thumb.

Her answering moan let him know it was what she needed. But he was getting closer to orgasm than she was, and he didn't know if he could hold his off any longer.

He stroked her back with his hands, running his fingers down her spine all the way to her butt, again and again. Each time, he drew closer to her anus until he let a finger linger there. Then, he pressed against the puckered area until the tip of his digit entered her as he continued thrusting inside her.

In no time at all, he felt her body tense. The moment she cried out his name, he gave in to the pleasure and let his climax take him.

Everything ceased to exist, but Kyra and the bliss they had found together. It was decadence at its finest, and he already craved more.

He pulled out of her and fell onto the bed. She scooted against him as he opened his arms for her. With their legs hanging over the side of the mattress, they wound their limbs together and simply lay in the silence of the room, each lost in the satisfaction they'd experienced.

"Wow," she murmured.

Dubhan smiled and rubbed his hand up and down her bare back. "I completely agree."

"We're going to do that again."

It wasn't a question, and he loved how straightforward she was with everything. "We most certainly are."

She smiled against his chest. "Good."

He wanted to languish in the aftermath of their lovemaking, but his mind drifted to the danger that now surrounded her. He'd brought it to her door. It was true that she hadn't had to help him, but he shouldn't have asked her. That was squarely on his shoulders.

Dubhan also wasn't sure how Eoghan or Death would react to Kyra. In fact, he was more than a little concerned about them finding out. But if he'd learned anything in his time with Death, it was that she always discovered everything eventually. There was no use hiding anything from her.

He drew in a deep breath, his gaze on the ceiling. Kyra's breathing had evened into sleep. He wished he could join her, but it was a luxury he could ill afford. Dubhan remained with her as long as he could before gently rolling her onto her other side so he could extricate his arm. He shifted her fully onto the bed and covered her before he walked into the living area, calling his clothes to him as he did.

After teleporting outside, he looked up at the sky and closed his eyes, searching for the same peace he'd discovered the night before. To his surprise, he found it. Dubhan held onto it for a moment longer, letting it seep into his body that was already relaxed after sex.

Then he opened his eyes and said, "Eoghan."

The Reaper leader arrived less than a minute later. He looked at Dubhan before glancing around, his quicksilver eyes lingering on the cottage before returning to Dubhan. "Did you find something?"

"Yes," Dubhan answered. "But not Xaneth. I actually stumbled upon something else entirely."

Eoghan waited silently.

Dubhan had fought many Fae in his life before and after becoming a Reaper, but he could honestly say he was glad that he'd never met Eoghan on the battlefield. There was a reason the Reaper was one of their leaders.

"Something in Drumshanbo kept me in the village," he told Eoghan. "I didn't realize what it was until I recognized that my wanderings kept leading me to a certain building. It's a bookstore owned by mortals."

Eoghan's forehead creased in a frown. "Why would humans draw your interest? Were they dealing with Fae?"

"Actually, it was the markings on the doorframe."

"What markings?"

Dubhan glanced at the moon. "The first was a symbol to keep Fae out."

"That's not uncommon here in Ireland. Especially if the family line goes back to when the Fae first arrived."

"I don't know about that. Honestly, I wasn't too concerned with the mortals keeping Fae out. It was the other symbol that caught my attention. One I'd seen only one other time in my life."

Eoghan raised his brows. "Where?"

"My parents' house."

Eoghan took that in, nodding slightly. "Do you know what the marking is?"

"I was never told."

Eoghan knew Dubhan's history. Reaper leaders knew the pasts of those they led to help them become a cohesive unit, so Dubhan didn't feel the need to elaborate.

"I see," Eoghan said after a moment.

Dubhan wished that was all he had to say. "There's more."

"There usually always is. I'm guessing it pertains to whoever occupies this cottage."

Dubhan gave a single nod. "I'll tell you how we came to meet, but first, I want you to know that I asked for her help in discovering what the symbol meant. When she went to find out, I veiled myself to follow her as she went to Belfast to ask a Fae couple there. They sent her to Maximillian."

Eoghan didn't utter a word, but his entire body tensed.

"I followed her through the Fae doorway to see him and was immediately dealt pain the likes of which I've never experienced."

"Not even a symbol to keep Fae out will stop us," Eoghan said.

Dubhan snorted. "He managed to find a marking to ward against Reapers."

Eoghan's lips parted at the news. "Is that so? But you managed to stay in his home?"

"It was excruciating, and I passed out afterwards, but yes, I did."

"I suppose you took the pain for a reason?"

Dubhan swallowed. "He knew what the symbol was I sought. He didn't want to tell Kyra at first, but she managed to get it out of him."

"Max doesn't tell anyone anything he doesn't want them to know."

"I believe he really didn't want to tell her. They were once lovers, and I think he still cares for her. He tried to talk her into forgetting about the symbol, but she wouldn't."

Eoghan grunted softly. "What did he tell her?"

"It's a symbol for the Others. More precisely, it's for those who are part of the Others, or those who want to join."

Eoghan's face went slack. "This is important information. I'm glad you looked into it."

Dubhan ran a hand down his face. "The couple Kyra went to, asking about the symbol? They were killed not long after she visited them."

"That isn't a coincidence."

"No, it isn't."

Eoghan's nostrils flared as he looked at the house. "Who is she?"

"A Light Fae."

Surprise filled Eoghan's face when he turned back to Dubhan.

"I know," Dubhan said. "The thing is, she was at the Light Castle when we fought the Trackers. Somehow, she was in the area of magic that Aisling put up so that no Fae could see the battle."

Eoghan simply sat there.

Worry knotted Dubhan's stomach. "She found me simply by thinking about me. In fact, she's been following me ever since the castle."

"She must be using some kind of magic."

Dubhan shook his head. "She does have an ancient spell book that her aunt found on the Fae Realm, but I looked in it. I think she's telling me the truth about how she found me."

"I don't like it, Dubhan. And Death isn't going to either."

Dubhan took a step toward Eoghan. "Without Kyra, we wouldn't know about the symbol. She's put her life in danger to help me."

"She knows what you are."

It wasn't a question. Dubhan glanced away and nodded. "She knows."

"I honestly don't know what Death's decision on this will be."

"I'd like to plead Kyra's case," Dubhan said.

Eoghan quirked a brow, surprise etched on his features. "You?"

"Yes."

"I'll see what I can do."

nine

Kyra didn't know what woke her. Her eyes flew open, her heart pounding.

"I heard it, too," Dubhan whispered from beside her.

She gripped his arm that was lying over her waist as he molded his body to hers from behind. Neither of them moved as they waited to hear the sound again, though she was acutely aware of how eerily silent the night was. Almost as if all the animals had simply . . . vanished.

Her body was tense, her blood pumping quickly. Every nerve screamed danger! She kept thinking about finding Tate and Jesta murdered. And of Max's warning. Was it the Others? Were they there to exact their revenge?

Kyra might know how to talk her way out of most things, but when it came to fight or flight—she was gone.

"Easy," Dubhan whispered in her ear.

She had no interest in meeting up with the Others since she had no intention of having her life ended. She didn't regret helping Dubhan, but she would only be a hindrance in battle.

Kyra parted her lips to tell him that when she heard a branch outside her window snap in two. With her heart beating double-time, she tried to decide what to do. Before she could, Dubhan had them on their feet and clothed. He turned her to look at him and put his finger to her lips. She nodded woodenly, too terrified to do much else.

Several tense minutes passed before the night came alive again. Whatever had been out there was gone. She should feel relieved. Instead, she couldn't stop thinking about what might have happened had Dubhan not been there.

He released her and took a step back.

"Where are you going?" she asked in a frantic whisper.

He calmly turned back to her. "I'm going to look outside. There might be some clue as to who was out there."

She winced when he used his normal voice, but she kept hers at a whisper. "We both know who it was."

"Maybe," Dubhan said with a shrug. "I won't know until I look. They're gone, Kyra."

"So you think. They could be out there waiting."

"If they wanted in, they would've gotten in," he told her.

She began to argue when she realized the truth of his words. Her mouth closed as she looked around her room. She no longer felt safe in the cottage. All these years, she'd believed that she had very few things she needed to worry about hurting her. The realization that there was a group like the Others out there, who also had it in for the Dragon Kings was terrifying.

How did a Fae like her—or any Fae, for that matter—combat such a group?

Dubhan's crimson gaze studied her. "I'm not leaving. I'm merely going for a look outside."

"I'll come with you," she said. That's when it dawned on her that she was no longer whispering, and she wasn't sure when she'd stopped.

Dubhan held out his hand. She took it, lacing her fingers with his. The moment their hands connected, some of her anxiety left. He gave her a nod. She smiled in return. Then they walked from the cottage together. Her senses were on high alert. She looked everywhere, but she realized she wasn't really seeing anything since she was only skimming things.

Kyra took a deep breath and looked to Dubhan to see what he was doing. He stood perfectly still, his head moving slowly from one side to the other as his eyes searched the darkness for any signs of an intruder.

He wasn't tense. In fact, he appeared relaxed, but that was likely only so he could react quickly if need be. She copied him, forcing herself to ease her muscles and calm down. Yet her fear still had her firmly in its grip.

And her desire to run far away from all of this was strong.

She made herself stand her ground. It was silly, this fear inside her. She'd never encountered anyone or anything where she was forced to defend herself using magic or battle skills before. It didn't help that all her life, her mother had drilled into her that women should let the men handle battle, while they took care of the home life.

So many years of that, and it had become ingrained in her to run at the first sign of conflict. Kyra had adjusted some over the years, and had gotten Eva's ability to talk her way out of tight situations, but this was entirely different.

Despite what was going on with her, Dubhan didn't seem the

least bit perturbed. That was probably because he was used to battle. It had nothing to do with him being Dark, and everything to do with him being in past scuffles.

His red eyes glanced her way. He said nothing as he started around the side of the house. She didn't want to go. In fact, her legs refused to budge at first, but she made her muscles obey her command and keep pace with Dubhan. He walked slowly, stopping and staring at the ground for several moments before his gaze moved around the area. He did that again and again until they reached her bedroom window.

She saw the broken twig the same time as Dubhan did. He squatted down beside it, releasing her hand so he could inspect the stick. After a few moments, he straightened and turned to her.

"That's a look of concern," she said.

His lips flattened briefly. "A Fae was here, but I don't know if it was a Light or a Dark. Does anyone know where you're staying?"

"No one."

"Hmm," he said and looked down the mountain to the village below. "There are several Fae down there."

She followed his gaze. "True, but I didn't interact with any of them."

"That doesn't mean one didn't follow you since you rode the motorbike instead of using magic."

Kyra frowned as she thought about her favorite mode of transportation. "I've been riding that for years. No Fae has been interested yet. Nor have any followed me."

"It's an option."

She gave him a flat look. "So are those who left those markings on the bookstore. We still don't know what they want."

"There's no need to think like that. It might have been someone else."

"I deal in facts," she stated. "Facts are what keep things simple and straightforward. Don't sugarcoat things because you don't believe I can handle it."

He blew out a breath. "You have a point, but I also saw your reaction to knowing someone was here."

"I'm working on that. The fact I'm still here says a lot."

"Yes, it does." He looked away, staring down the mountain for a long, silent minute. Then he faced her and said, "It could've been the Others. It also could have been someone else. For all I know, it was a Reaper."

That stunned her. She hadn't even considered that possibility. "Do you often sneak up on your fellow Reapers?"

"No. Nor would they have come and not called for me."

"So, we're back to the Others or those who wish to join them."

He grinned. "Do you always think the worst?"

"It's safer that way."

"Even if it was the Others, they wouldn't have gotten to you."

She raised her brows. "You've fought them before?"

"Not exactly."

Which meant that he had no idea if he could stand against them. Kyra didn't point that out. It wasn't in her nature to make others feel small or stupid, so she kept her thoughts to herself.

"Do you know how I became a Reaper?" he suddenly asked.

She was game for anything to take her mind off those after her, and her potential death. She shook her head. "How?"

"I had to die. Violently, and through betrayal. I earned my spot with the Reapers because of my ability to fight."

Kyra gaped at him, her mind not quite able to take in what he was saying. "You died?"

His nostrils flared. "Death chooses us carefully. We are offered our souls in exchange for service."

"How long do you serve?"

"Until we die again."

Kyra swallowed, her brow furrowing. "But you were brought back."

"That's right, but it isn't something Death can do—or will do—again. We get one chance. I don't know of anyone who turned down the opportunity to become a Reaper. Not only do we get a second chance, but we're serving a higher power."

"I've seen you move. All of you. You're much more than just Fae."

"That's true. We get a drop of Death's powers. That makes us faster, our senses greater, our magic stronger, and we can remain veiled for as long as we want."

The knowledge that she had been following him around, thinking she was fooling him made her look silly. It was a wonder that Dubhan hadn't smote her on the spot. Kyra drew in a steadying breath. "Why are you telling me this?"

"I wouldn't have, but you saw me and followed me. You also helped me. I feel it's only fair that you know something."

She gave him a guarded look, her eyes narrowing. "I don't know anyone who knew of the Reapers. Most Fae wouldn't even discuss you. And even when you and I spoke, you went out of your way not to state you were a Reaper. I'm guessing there was a reason for that. Like, perhaps I'm not supposed to know."

His stare was answer enough.

"I see. What does it mean for me now that I know?"

"We have one rule. No one can know of us. If any discover the truth, they die."

Well, she did ask. Kyra really needed to learn to keep her mouth shut. Sometimes, it was better not knowing everything. "I'm going to die."

"I don't want to give you false hope, but I plan to speak to Death on your behalf."

Kyra was stunned by his declaration. "Why would you do that?"

"You helped me. I'm going to help you."

She wanted to believe it was because he might feel something for her, but Kyra knew better than to assume anything. No doubt his thinking was as simple as his statement had been. He was helping her because she'd helped him.

"Thanks. I appreciate it. But should you?" she asked.

His brows snapped together as the wind ruffled his hair. "What is that supposed to mean?"

"The Others will likely be coming for me. You and I both know it after what they did to Jesta and Tate."

"We don't know for sure that it was them."

"And we don't know that it wasn't. Max was frightened enough to keep himself hidden away. That tells me I need to take it seriously."

Dubhan snorted and looked away, derision marking his face. "Maximillian lies."

"We've been over this. I know Max lies, but I believe him on this." The longer she stared at Dubhan's profile, the more she got the feeling that he knew something more.

"You don't like Max."

Dubhan gave a single shake of his head.

Kyra got a sick feeling in her stomach, one that she prayed her hyper-imagination had gotten wrong. "Did you go to Max for something."

"Obviously," came Dubhan's reply.

That had been evident, but she hadn't been able to get out the question she really wanted to ask. Now, though, it was either ask it or let it go—and she couldn't let it go. "Was he part of your betrayal?"

"He wasn't part of it. He set up the entire thing."

CHAPTER

ten

"Dubhan did what?" Cael asked, his voice laced with astonishment.

Erith sat on the bench inside the white tower with Cael and watched Eoghan as he related all that Dubhan had told him about Kyra, the symbol, and the Others.

"It's out of character for Dubhan," Eoghan said as he stood before them.

"Is it?" she asked.

Both men looked at her. Erith swung her gaze from Eoghan's liquid silver eyes to Cael's purple ones. Both she and Cael were learning his new abilities together, and each day, he surprised her with what he could do now. Sometimes, she still couldn't believe that she had found the love she had so desperately yearned for. But find it she had.

Eoghan cleared his throat. "Dubhan wants to plead Kyra's case."

Erith swung her head back to Eoghan as Cael wound a strand

of her long, blue-black hair around his finger. "It was a lot easier when things were cut and dried for all of you, but it isn't that simple anymore."

"You're Death," Cael stated. "You can do whatever you want."

"That doesn't mean I should," she answered with a grin.

His lips curved into a smile. "And that's one of the many reasons I love you."

She reached beside her on the bench and put her hand on Cael's thigh as she turned her attention to Eoghan. "I'm more than a little concerned about how she was able to find Dubhan. We need to know how she did it, because if it was with magic, then that can be taught to others."

"Dubhan doesn't think that's the case," Eoghan said.

Cael snorted. "Dubhan is thinking with his cock."

"You're not wrong," Eoghan said with a knowing grin.

Death rolled her eyes. "If Dubhan is willing to stick his neck out for this female, then she must be important. Do I also need to point out that Dubhan isn't exactly the kind who asks for help? Have either of you realized that he could've come to us to help him learn what the symbol was? Instead, he asked Kyra."

"I'm very aware of that," Eoghan stated. There was no anger in his tone, but he wasn't pleased in the least.

Erith sighed. "From what Dubhan has told you, Kyra didn't hesitate to help. And Dubhan followed her?"

"He did," Eoghan said. "Though he said it was to make sure she was safe, not because he didn't trust her."

Cael's brows shot up on his forehead. "That says a lot about what Dubhan feels for this Fae. And she's Light?"

"She is," Eoghan said with a nod.

Erith didn't care about that. Her interest was focused on other things. "Dubhan went to Maximillian's?"

Eoghan threw up his hands in disbelief. "He did."

"And he didn't kill Max?"

"I don't know if it was because of the symbol Max used to keep Reapers out, or if Dubhan managed to control himself. But, no, he didn't go after Max."

Erith glanced at Cael. "That's a feat in itself."

"It is," Cael agreed.

"This symbol Max has for the Reapers," she said, "we need to know who created it."

Eoghan shrugged. "I'm betting Max did, but I'll look into it."

"Have Dubhan do it."

Her statement caused both men to stare at her in astonishment.

"Why would you put him in such a situation?" Eoghan asked. "You know how Dubhan feels about Max."

Cael didn't give her time to answer before he said, "You've always allowed my group to take their revenge on those who betrayed them."

She wasn't in the habit of explaining herself, but then again, she wasn't ruling alone anymore either. Since Cael now had a healthy dose of her magic, he was her equal. In order for their relationship to work, they had to share all things.

"It's true, I've given some Reapers the boon of getting revenge on those who killed them. I didn't with Dubhan because Max is the answer for many Fae who have nowhere else to turn. Many times, his lies—as horrible as they are—are also the answers those Fae need."

"Dubhan isn't going to like that reason," Eoghan cautioned.

A muscle jumped in Cael's jaw. "Because it's shite, and we all know it."

Erith rolled her eyes. "If I had let Dubhan kill Max all those years ago, there wouldn't have been anyone around now to tell Kyra or Dubhan about the symbol or its meaning."

"It's still a shite reason," Cael stated.

Erith knew it was, but she didn't have any other option. "Dubhan will be able to get his revenge eventually."

"I think Erith might have made the right move," Eoghan said.

Cael made a sound in the back of his throat. "What?"

Eoghan held up his hand to stop his friend from speaking. "Hear me out. We were able to go after those who wronged us not long after we were turned into Reapers. Did taking that revenge heal us?"

Erith looked at Cael, but he didn't answer.

Eoghan then continued. "Hearing that Dubhan was able to stand in the same room with Max and not attack him, shows that Dubhan might be putting the past to rest."

Erith thought about what Max had done to Dubhan, and she knew that wasn't the case, but she held her tongue for the moment.

"What are you going to do about Kyra?" Cael asked her.

Erith looked up. "I've made a lot of concessions for those who have helped us. Rhi, Balladyn, Xaneth. They all knew about the Reapers, and I allowed them to live. The women who have found love with Reapers aided us because they helped when it was most needed."

"Are you giving Kyra that same distinction?" Eoghan asked.

"I'm waiting to pass judgment. I want to see what happens next, and I would like to talk to Dubhan myself," she said. "Besides, we need to get to the real matter at hand. The Others."

Cael put his hand over hers where it rested on his thigh. "We need to get this new information Kyra and Dubhan discovered to Con and the Dragon Kings immediately."

"Yes, we do," Erith replied. She hadn't spoken to Con or any of the Kings since Usaeil had been killed. There was much she wanted to ask the King of Dragon Kings, but there was also a lot that he might want to keep private.

Eoghan interrupted her thoughts. "There's also the matter of the Others coming after Kyra."

"That's not going to happen," Erith declared. "Eoghan, send Aisling and Rordan to the herbal shop in Belfast. I want proof it was the Others who killed the Fae couple."

Eoghan gave a nod. "Anything else?"

"Send Cathal to Maximillian. I want to know what Cathal can pull out of Max. Keep the rest searching for Xaneth." She knew finding the royal Light Fae was probably a long shot, but she owed Xaneth, and she intended to keep looking for him.

After Eoghan had left, Cael got to his feet and went to pour himself some gin and her a glass of red wine. He returned, handing her the wine glass.

"You don't agree with my decision regarding Dubhan and Max?" she asked.

He shrugged and sat back, putting one arm along the back of the bench. "I don't disagree. I definitely think a visit to Max is in order. I tend to agree with Kyra that it was the Others who killed the Fae couple in Belfast, but that's simply because I don't believe in coincidences."

"No," Erith said with a sigh. "I don't either. But the Others reacted quickly. If they're around—which they apparently are—why haven't they attacked the Kings since that is their main goal? Or is this an entirely different group we're dealing with?"

Cael took a drink of the gin. "I think they're waiting on something. Think about all the Dragon Kings have been through with things the Others put into place thousands of years ago. The

Others are nothing if not patient. And you're right, there could be another group."

"But the Druids involved in the original group are long gone. Even the Fae could be dead by now. But if there are others…"

"The Kings and Rhi haven't been able to find anything."

She looked away and drank her wine. "I've always kept my focus on the Fae."

"That's not true. Need I remind you of the times you visited Con in the guise of helping him?"

Erith brought Cael's hand to her lips and kissed it. "I love you."

"I love you, too," he said and pulled her toward him so she reclined against his side. "There's still the matter of Kyra being in danger. Shall I pull my Reapers from collecting souls?"

She shook her head. "Let them have more downtime. They may not have it much longer, and they've been through so much. I thought you and I could keep an eye on Kyra. Because I'd like to get an up-close view of the Others."

"I do like the way you think," Cael said and kissed the top of her head.

"I'd rather you be kissing other parts of me."

He chuckled and sat up as he set aside his glass. He took her hand as he got to his feet and drew her with him to the stairs of the tower that led to their bedroom. "All I ever want to do is kiss you, all over. I'm certainly not going to turn down that offer."

"We do have several millennia to make up for," she said as they ran up the stairs.

"Damn straight." He then stopped, gathered her in his arms, and teleported them to their bedroom.

Erith removed their clothes with a thought, and they fell onto the bed in a tangle of lips and limbs.

Maximillian stared at the Fae doorway. He etched in more of the markings keeping out Reapers and those associated with the Others. One wasn't enough. Someone had come through the doorway with Kyra, he was sure of it.

Either she hadn't known, or Kyra had lied to him. She was a great liar, so he couldn't be sure which one it was. Regardless, he was going to ensure that there were no other surprises like that again.

Mostly, he regretted what he'd told Kyra. He should've lied. He should've told her anything but the truth. Why had he believed that if she knew the facts, that it might change her mind? Max shook his head, wishing he could turn back time and change what he'd told her about the symbol.

Kyra made sure to get far away from any type of physical conflict, but she was just stubborn enough to believe she could outsmart the Others and stay safe. But Max knew differently.

"Oh, Kyra," he murmured as he deepened the symbol he was marking on the doorway.

If there had ever been anyone he could've loved, it would've been Kyra. In fact, he was sure he had fallen in love with her. Then she'd left him. That had been a particularly difficult blow—and a very bad time in his life.

He had told numerous lies to so many people. Some to keep them out of danger, but those had been the minority. Mostly, he told lies because he didn't know the truth. And he liked getting paid. He'd discovered quickly that people didn't check to see if what he told them was true. They simply paid and left.

The few who returned looking for retribution had been swiftly dealt with.

And then there was that one Dark. He'd never forget the Fae's face, but the name escaped Max. The Dark's own family had wanted him gone, and they had paid Max to not only come up with the plan, but to facilitate things, as well. The sheer amount of money he'd made off that deal had set him up for dozens of centuries.

Max had never hesitated in lying to others. It came naturally. A few times, he would give the truth just to keep people guessing whether he was a liar or might have just gotten something wrong.

But the only time he had ever had a hand in sending someone to their death was that Dark Fae. That haunted him to this day. For all Max knew, he might be joining that Dark soon, because he had a feeling that no matter what he did, the Others would find him.

CHAPTER
eleven

No matter how hard he tried to forget the past, it was always there, waiting to kick his feet out from under him. Dubhan knew this, and yet every time, he couldn't right himself. This time was no different. Even though he was the one who'd told Kyra the truth about Max.

Whether he brought up the past, or it rose up on its own, it still knocked him sideways. When would it loosen its hold? When would it stop interrupting his life?

"Max did what?" Kyra asked softly. Her eyes were wide, her face slack from disbelief.

Dubhan had wanted to shock her, but mostly, he wanted her to know that Max wasn't the man she believed him to be. However, now that Dubhan had said the words, he wanted to take them back. It wasn't right that he transferred his pain onto Kyra. She didn't deserve that.

"It doesn't matter."

Kyra moved to step in front of him when he tried to turn

away. "It most certainly does. I knew Max had done some questionable things, but . . . I didn't know he would stoop so low. I'm sorry."

Dubhan was taken aback that she would think she needed to apologize. "You've done nothing to be sorry for."

"I disagree. I knew Max. If by nothing more than being connected to him, I owe you an apology."

He turned her, putting his hand on her back as he walked her into the cottage. "Maximillian is responsible for his sins. Not you."

"Can you tell me what he did exactly? Not that it matters. Just knowing he was instrumental in your betrayal and death is enough to make sure I never speak to him again."

"You may have to talk to him again. Whether we like it or not, Max finds his way to knowing certain things. I'll just have to make sure he doesn't lie the next time we see him."

Kyra's lips turned up in a grin. "I like the way you think." Then she frowned.

"What?" Dubhan asked.

"Two things. One, can you speak to him? Won't he realize what you are—which would mean his death?"

"Would you think less of me if I said yes."

She shook her head. "Max deserves whatever is coming to him after what he did to you. If finding out you're a Reaper means his death, then so be it."

Dubhan wanted to smile, but he kept it locked inside. Her words pleased him more than she could ever know. Being around her, having her involved in everything was doing something to him. The attraction was deepening, becoming something he wasn't sure he could shake.

If he even wanted to try.

"And the second?"

"How will we determine if he's lying or not? Max is a master at it."

"I'll remain with him while you check whatever it is he tells us. If he's lying, he won't do it to anyone again. But all this could be a moot point. We may not have to go to him again."

Kyra twisted her lips as she sighed loudly. "I hope you're right, but I've got a feeling we will see Max again."

Dubhan was amazed by Kyra. She found the good in every situation. It was something new and entirely foreign to him, and yet he liked the idea of it. He wasn't sure he could do the same, but he'd like to try.

"What?" she asked.

Dubhan realized he'd been staring. He cleared his throat. "You're different than anyone I know."

"You've just been hanging with the wrong people," she said with a wink.

He chuckled, thinking of his fellow Reapers. Each of them had their own issues, but then again, that tended to happen when a person was betrayed and murdered. None of that just went away when Death approached them.

"Do you think whoever was outside will be back?" Kyra asked with a small frown.

Dubhan nodded, thinking of the lack of anything he'd found around the house. "I'm not leaving you, though."

"You're still looking for Xaneth."

"Then come with me."

Her lips curved into a smile. "I can do that?"

"Of course."

"Good. I've always liked puzzles, and it seems like locating Xaneth is right up my alley."

Dubhan watched as she walked to the kitchen and put water in the kettle. She was a Fae and could do most everything she wanted with magic—as most Fae could. But, apparently, not Kyra. She took a mortal's approach to everyday life.

She looked up and laughed as she put the kettle on the stove. "I grew up using magic for everything. It wasn't until I was with my aunt that I saw her doing mundane things like this. I asked her why, and she told me that she found a certain kind of contentment when doing such things. I didn't understand then."

He remained silent as her gaze took on a faraway look. Then she seemed to shake herself and turn on the stove before her silver gaze slid to him.

"Once Eva died, I found myself searching for anything to help me get through it. I was so angry, I smashed a teacup of hers that happened to be her favorite." Kyra smiled at him, but it was full of sadness. "I, of course, fixed it with magic, but it made me think of how precious she found such things. After that, I tried doing a few things here and there that I'd seen her do without magic. Oddly enough, it helped. The anger within me began to dissipate, and before long, I was doing less and less magic. You may not believe this, but I feel like it actually gave me more power for when I do use magic."

"I can see that," he said. "You cared a great deal for your aunt. What happened to her?"

"I don't know. She's just . . . gone."

He frowned, confused. "Gone? Then why did you say she was dead?"

"Because Eva would never leave like that. Something happened to her. Over a century ago. I looked all over this realm and spoke to everyone I knew, but I never found her."

"A puzzle you didn't solve."

Kyra twisted her lips. "Exactly. When I saw you fight at the

Light Castle and knew you had to be a Reaper, I began following you in the hopes you might help me discover what happened to Eva."

"You never asked," he told her with a frown. And the more he thought about it, the more he wondered why she hadn't.

Kyra shrugged her shoulders and looked away. "I was going to." Her silver eyes slid back to his. "But when we spoke, I knew I couldn't ask for anything right away. I'd planned to see if you could help me when we finished your puzzle. Besides, yours is much more important than mine."

"I didn't mean to make you think you couldn't ask me about your aunt."

"It's fine," she assured him with a smile. "We've got time."

Dubhan didn't point out that she had yet to find her aunt. Sometimes, it was better to leave things unsaid. He wanted to help Kyra, and this was why Death wanted the Reapers' identities kept secret, so no one could ask for such a favor.

The kettle whistled. Kyra took it off the stove and poured the steaming water into two mugs. She went about fixing her tea, and all the while, he couldn't stop looking at her. Her movements were fluid, practiced, and there was a sense of contentment about her that he hadn't noticed before.

Maybe it was her peace that seeped into him. Whatever it was, he liked it. She made him look at everything differently, to consider all possibilities instead of being rigid in his thoughts and actions.

And for some reason, that made him think of the past. Before he knew it, the words were out of his mouth.

"I never told you what Max did."

She shoved her black hair from her face, and as she did, it shifted to a deep purple that faded to blueish green. The length remained the same, just brushing the tops of her shoulders. "You don't need to tell me if you'd rather not talk about it."

"I want to." And he did, strangely enough.

Kyra walked to him and took his hand before pulling him toward the sofa. She gave him a little push, so he sat. Then she returned to the kitchen to retrieve the mugs before curling up next to him.

Dubhan accepted the tea, not having the heart to tell her he couldn't stand the stuff. Funny how he didn't hesitate to speak his mind with anyone else, but when it came to Kyra, he kept such things to himself. It might have been different had she asked if he wanted tea instead of assuming.

He looked down at the liquid as his thoughts turned back to that fateful night. "I told you I was raised to follow orders without asking questions. If any of us dared, we quickly felt my father's fist."

"That's not a good way to grow up."

"It's all I knew. I believed everyone was like that for the longest time. A few times, I stepped out of line and didn't move quite right or quick enough, and I was rewarded with a beating. My father didn't believe in forgiveness. Said that you didn't give mercy to anyone. To him, anyone who did those things was weak, and he wanted to make sure his sons weren't weak."

Kyra sipped her tea, holding the mug between her hands. "And your mother? What did she think?"

"The same as my father. Other Dark gave us a wide berth. My father said it was because they feared us, and that made him happy. I fell in line like my four brothers, doing everything that was expected of me. Until one day, I was sent out with my youngest brother. We were less than a year apart in age, but we never got along."

Kyra touched his arm briefly and smiled warmly. "I didn't get along with my sister either."

"This was different. He liked delivering pain. So did my older brothers, but not with as much glee as my younger brother did."

"And you?" Kyra asked.

Dubhan thought about that for a moment before he shrugged. "I had a duty. I did it without thinking, without feeling. It was how I was taught. But that day, I watched my sibling attack a bird simply because he wanted to. He tortured it until I couldn't take it anymore. I shoved him away from the animal and put the bird out of its misery. He didn't say a word to me, nor me to him. We went about our day and completed the job my father had sent us to do. Weeks passed. If I came into the room with my family, I got the feeling that they had been talking about me. They were never warm and loving, but there was a different . . . coldness about them after that."

"Did you think of just leaving?"

He nodded before he lifted the cup to his lips and drank without thinking about it. He was surprised to find that he liked the taste. Dubhan ended up taking several drinks before he spoke. "Every day, actually. That's not the plan my father had for us. For generations, my family had set practices. The children remained with the parents, doing all the chores until they found spouses. Only then could they leave their parents' houses."

"You're kidding?" she asked, mouth agape.

"Like I said, it was all I knew."

"How were you supposed to meet anyone if you didn't have some time to yourself? Or did you have time to yourself?"

He shook his head. "Not really. We had a little, but I wasn't content with that. I began to take notice of other families and people when we were out. When I was sent on missions alone, I took extra time just to be by myself."

Kyra's brows drew together. "Missions?"

Dubhan briefly closed his eyes as he turned his head away. "I was Dark."

"Yes," she said softly. Then she put her hand on his arm.

And this time, she left it.

Dubhan turned his face to her. "One week, I was sent with one of my other brothers on a mission, but we had to get information from Maximillian first. Max gave one item to my brother, but he told me that I had to go to another place to get the other. I knew he was lying, but I wasn't sure why. I didn't question him. Instead, I left. As soon as I arrived at the location, my family was waiting for me."

Kyra took his cup and set both hers and his aside. Then she climbed into his lap and wrapped her arms around him. It took a moment before he returned her embrace. She said nothing, simply held him. As he sat there, feeling her energy surrounding him, he realized that the pain he usually felt when thinking of that night wasn't as great as it had been before.

He didn't know how Kyra had done it, but he could almost imagine that she was healing the scars of that betrayal. It was absurd.

And yet, he knew it was the truth.

CHAPTER
twelve

Kyra didn't realize one person could hold so much pain inside them. Though she normally tried not to feel the pain of others, she searched for Dubhan's now. But opening herself up to such emotions was . . . dangerous. The torment fell around her like a suffocating blanket that threatened to smother her. Instantly, the magic she kept hidden from others rose up and began shifting the pain, drawing it out of Dubhan and into herself. He needed to find peace, and if she could help him achieve that, then she would do it.

She was appalled that anything so heinous could be done to a person by their family regardless if they were Dark or not. And to know that Max was involved. . . . She knew Max. He would've gotten all the details as to why they wanted him to help, so he would've known exactly what he was doing.

Kyra closed her eyes as her body grew heavy from taking on so much pain. It wasn't something she did often because the recovery grew longer each time she did it. It was a gift from her father's side of the family, one that none of her sisters had gotten. Kyra treasured her ability, but it also made her acutely aware of others' pain to such a degree that she wanted to help everyone.

And was why she often kept to herself. Because she'd learned the hard way that not everyone wanted help.

It became impossible to keep her head up. She rested her cheek on Dubhan's head, but she wasn't there for long. He shifted them so she was lying across his lap as he held her in his arms. She looked up into his deep red eyes and smiled before she ran her fingers through his black and silver hair.

"What did you do?" he asked, curiosity sparking in his crimson depths.

"I helped rid you of some of the pain. Perhaps I should've asked, but you've carried it long enough."

He stared at her, shock reverberating through him. "By the stars. You're one of those Kavanaughs. I thought the Kavanaugh story was a myth, but it's real."

"What do you mean?" she asked worriedly.

"I've heard of your family, Kyra. Your line has the ability to take away pain, whether from the body or the spirit. I know there are Dark who have wanted to capture one of you."

Somehow, that didn't surprise her. It made her wonder if that's why her aunt had disappeared. As quickly as she thought it, it was gone. If Eva had the ability to take away pain, she would've told Kyra.

"You look ill," Dubhan said.

She shrugged and closed her eyes as she dropped her hand to her lap. "It takes a while for what I've absorbed to filter through me."

"You absorb it?" he asked in a soft voice. "Does that mean it's . . . in you?"

She nodded since talking took too much effort.

His hold on her tightened. "Do you carry it with you always, or does it leave?"

"Some of it leaves."

"Thank you," he said and kissed her forehead. "But I am not worth you harming yourself."

She forced her eyes open to look at him. "You most certainly are worth it. You're more worthy than anyone I've ever known."

A muscle moved in his jaw, but he didn't say anything else. For the next hour, he simply held her, letting her drift between sleep and wakefulness until she was able to keep her eyes open.

"How do you know how much to take from someone?" he asked.

She tried to get off his lap, but he tightened his hold, refusing to let her move. "I don't. I let my body tell me when it's had too much. Then I stop."

"Don't tell others what you can do. People will use it for their benefit."

"I get to choose who I help," she said.

He shook his head. "You've not encountered the worst of this realm. The ones who manipulate and lie to get what they want, all while making you believe it was your idea the whole time."

"I guess I've been fortunate, then."

"Very much so." He shook his head, his lips thinning. "When I think about what could've happened to you. . . ."

"Don't," she told him. "I'm fine. I'm here with you, unhurt."

His crimson eyes met hers. "I'm very thankful for that."

"We've wasted enough time. Let's start looking for Xaneth."

"I've been all over Drumshanbo. He's not here."

She rolled her eyes. "There are lots of places you haven't looked."

"I'm thorough."

"I'm not implying that you aren't, but there are some places that need a deeper look. Not to mention the bookshop."

He stood, putting her on her feet as he did. "You can't get near it, remember?"

She cocked a brow. "Maybe not me, but someone needs to visit that place."

"It isn't going to be you. Or me, for that matter."

"I can acknowledge when someone points out something I overlooked. Besides, I'd very much like to stay alive since I'm not nearly done exploring that gorgeous body of yours."

Dubhan grinned and drew her against him, lacing his arms around her once more. "That's a good thing since I plan on doing much more to you."

"Is that right?" she asked with a teasing glint in her eye. "I'm definitely up for that."

"Just wait. There's so much more."

She raised her brows. "It's all I'll be thinking about now."

"That's exactly what I wanted to hear."

"Oh," she said and playfully punched him in the arm. "That's not fair."

"It is since every time I look at you, all I can think about is kissing you, which makes me think of how beautiful you are when you come."

Her body clenched with need at his words. She was breathless when she said, "You really do need to stop."

"Never."

"Is that a promise?" she asked with a grin.

He gave a nod. "It is."

She really could get used to this. Dubhan might have carried a substantial load of pain and anger, but despite it all—or perhaps because of it—he hadn't allowed it to destroy him like it would have others. It showed his strength of character, something that Death must have also taken note of.

Her smile dropped as she thought about a future with Dubhan, one she hadn't imagined until that moment. But she wanted more with him, desperately, but how could she have that when he was a Reaper and owed his life to Death? There was no room in his world for her.

"You're sad," he said, a frown marring his face.

She forced a smile and rose up on her toes to place her lips against his. "I'm happy being with you."

"Don't lie, remember?"

Kyra looked away and drew in a deep breath before releasing it. Only then did she meet his gaze. "I knew when I first saw you at the Light Castle that you were special. I didn't realize how much so until I met you. I thought I followed you because you could help me find Eva. But even that took a backseat as all I wanted to do was be near you, talk to you. Then it happened. And you were . . . so much more than I could've ever hoped for. I didn't expect to fall so hard for you."

"Fall for me?" he repeated in a low voice as his eyes searched hers.

She swallowed and continued talking while trying not to notice that he was shocked at her words. "I just realized that I have limited time with you, and I want to make the most of it."

"Kyra," he began.

"If you aren't going to let me go to the bookstore, then we need to find someone who can and will. I think I know someone who might do it."

"Who?"

She grinned up at him. "A mortal. A teenager looking to make a quick, easy bit of money. I figure he's our best bet."

"Why would you trust him? He could work for the Others or those looking to join them."

"Maybe he does. We won't know until we ask."

Dubhan gave her a hard look. "We wouldn't even know then since neither of us is entering the bookstore."

"Yikes. Good point," she said and wrinkled her nose. "Come meet him. You can decide if we ask him to do this or not."

Dubhan nodded. "Where is he?"

"He's always near the library, trying to hustle people."

"Fun," Dubhan said in a dry tone.

Kyra laughed. "He's quite good, actually. You'll like him."

"It's nearly dawn. Let's go have a look at some of the other places you were talking about before we find your fellow."

She didn't even get a chance to reply before he teleported them to the village. Obviously, he had no interest in getting on her motorbike, which was too bad because she was sure he'd like the speed.

"Where to?" Dubhan asked.

The streets were just beginning to come alive. She wondered why Dubhan had landed them near the pub where he'd confronted her, but she soon realized that he was veiled, and since he had hold of her hand, so was she.

"I like this," she said, looking at him.

He grinned but put his finger to his lips. She inwardly grimaced. She'd never stayed veiled long enough to realize that while others might not be able to see them, they could hear them. Actually, she wasn't sure if any other Fae outside of the Reapers knew that since the Fae couldn't hold a veil for long at all.

Dubhan nudged her. Kyra turned and began walking. He fell in step with her, their fingers laced as they strolled down the street. It was nice to have him beside her. For a little while, she could pretend that they were a couple out and about for a stroll.

Then they reached the church. Dubhan frowned, but she pulled him after her as she entered through a door in the back and went down several flights of stairs. They explored the underground until he was satisfied that there was nothing out of the ordinary there.

After that, they checked a building on the outskirts of the village that was being renovated—a set of flats, and a hidden room upstairs in a pub.

And yet, they still found nothing.

Kyra was more than disappointed. She'd really hoped that Dubhan would discover something that would help him find Xaneth.

"I'm not the only one searching," he told her when no one was near enough to hear. "There are others looking for Xaneth, as well."

She glanced at him. "That's good, but this realm is rather large, as you know. How many Reapers are there?"

He shrugged. "Not enough, apparently."

Kyra chuckled at his sarcasm but realized he hadn't answered the question. She didn't press, though. "I'm sorry there was nothing."

"Actually, the fact there wasn't anything here was something. We can now mark this village off and move on to the next."

Kyra wondered if she'd get to go with Dubhan when he left. They hadn't spoken of the future, and she wasn't sure how to bring it up. Or even if she should.

The more she thought about it, the more she thought that it was better if she just accepted whatever time she had with

Dubhan. It could be ten hours, ten days, ten months, or ten centuries.

"Let's go find your mortal," Dubhan said.

Kyra could hardly contain her excitement. She wanted to know what was in the bookstore, and she hoped Dubhan liked the youth enough to let him go in. Kyra had enough money to make it worth the mortal's time.

"You're frowning again."

She glanced at Dubhan and smoothed her brow. "I was just thinking that the young man won't have a clue as to what we're looking for. He could stare right at it and not realize we need to know about it."

"I've been thinking about that. Humans carry their mobile phones everywhere. He could use it to record the store so we could look at it at our leisure."

"That's brilliant."

Dubhan beamed before using glamour to hide his red eyes and the silver in his hair. "Thanks."

She wondered how many people had told him he'd done good in his life. Knowing how he had been brought up, she suspected that number was very low.

Her thoughts halted as they reached the library, and she found the mortal lounging on the steps, rolling a cigarette.

CHAPTER
thirteen

"I knew you'd be back," said the young human to Kyra with a cocky smile before raking his hands through his short, blond hair.

Dubhan had seen many sides of mortals. The young, he noticed, were more confident and assertive than the older generations. He suspected that it was because the young hadn't yet realized what they had at stake—or what could be taken from them.

Kyra didn't return the youth's smile. Instead, she cut her silver eyes to the boy and replied, "What makes you think I'm here for you."

"Why else would you be at the library?" His dark brown gaze raked up and down Kyra. "You don't seem the type who needs books. Especially when you have Muscles with you." Mike tipped his head at Dubhan.

Dubhan decided it was time he intervened. "My name is Dubhan. I gather you have a name?"

The youth turned his gaze to Dubhan and shrugged. "Maybe. Why should I give it to you?"

"We have a job we're considering you for. Kyra thinks you'd be perfect for it. Me? I'm not convinced."

The young man grinned and nodded as he glanced at Kyra. "You should trust her. She can spot a good one."

Kyra rolled her eyes. "And you're so humble."

The mortal shrugged. "In this world, if you don't make your stand and give yourself the pats on the back, no one else will."

Dubhan liked the human. Kyra was right, he would be the perfect person to go into the bookstore.

"Well?" the youth asked as he looked between them. "I'm your man."

Kyra snorted and crossed her arms over her chest. "You don't even know what we want you to do."

"I won't kill or hurt anyone. Other than that, I consider each job on the merits provided."

Dubhan noted how skinny the mortal was. "When was the last time you ate?"

The mortal suddenly didn't want to talk. He shrugged and looked away. "I ate."

Dubhan eyed the youth. He suspected that the mortal hadn't had an easy childhood, but that could be said for many humans. "Why do you sit out here on these steps instead of finding a job?"

"I'm looking for a job, but it isn't easy when you haven't finished schooling. I've got street smarts, and that's what I use to my advantage," the young man stated, raising his chin, defiance in his dark eyes.

Dubhan didn't say anything as he met Kyra's gaze before nodding toward a nearby café.

Kyra turned to the youth. "We're going to have some breakfast. If you'd care to learn about our job offer, you're welcome to join us."

Neither of them looked back as they turned and walked to the restaurant. They had barely gotten a table when the mortal arrived, his fingers thrust into the front pockets of his jeans. Dubhan held out his hand to one of the other two vacant chairs, and the youth sat.

"My friends call me Mike."

"Nice to meet you, Mike," Dubhan said. "Order whatever you want."

Kyra met Mike's gaze. "However much you want, and whatever you want."

"Why are you two being so nice?" Mike asked skeptically.

Dubhan shrugged and looked at the menu. "It's good to have a healthy dose of mistrust for people."

"I can't tell you how many times people have tried to fek me over." He glanced at Kyra. "Sorry. Screwed me over."

She didn't bat an eye—or look up from the menu—when she said, "That's fekking horrible."

Dubhan hid his smile when Mike sat back, becoming more comfortable. He had yet to figure the mortal out. Was the youth giving them a load of shite to make them feel sorry for him? It was a possibility. Mike could be telling the truth, but Dubhan suspected that most of what fell from the human's lips was lies as he did his best to keep food in his belly and a roof over his head.

"This is a small village. I bet you know most everyone," Dubhan said.

Mike shrugged one shoulder. "Tourists stand out. It makes them easy targets."

"What about me?" Kyra said.

His dark gaze slid to her. "You intrigued me. You weren't a local, but you weren't a tourist either. I'm not sure why you're here. Maybe visiting friends. You aren't like any other."

"You wouldn't believe me if I told you what I was," she said with a grin.

Dubhan narrowed his eyes at Mike as the human's stare grew intense. Some mortals knew of the Fae. There weren't many, but those that did, knew of his kind because they had some type of interaction with the Fae, whether it be just talking, or sex. The only reason Mike and everyone else wasn't currently falling all over Kyra or Dubhan was because they'd made sure to mask the very thing that drew mortals to them like moths to a flame.

"Try me," Mike urged.

Dubhan met Kyra's gaze. He wouldn't tell the mortal what they were, but he also wasn't going to tell Kyra what to do. If she wanted Mike to know that she was Fae, then that was her choice.

Kyra eyed Mike for a long moment before she crossed her arms on the table and leaned forward. "All right. I'll tell you."

They were interrupted by the waitress. Kyra and Dubhan chose their meals, each getting a large plate. When it came time for Mike to order, the youth didn't hesitate to do the same.

"I'm waiting," Mike said when they were alone once more.

Kyra's smile disappeared. "It's not a glamorous story. The truth is that I'm after an ex-boyfriend who ran off with quite a bit of my money. We've," she said, nodding to Dubhan, "tracked him here to a bookstore. However, he knows us, and we can't go in to make sure he's there so I can confront him."

"That's what you need me for?" Mike asked as he rested an arm on the table.

Dubhan nodded as he looked around the café just to be safe.

"We'd like you to video your arrival and interactions with anyone there, but also try to get a view of everything in the store."

"It's not just the ex-lover you're after, is it?" Mike said with a knowing smile.

Dubhan jerked his chin to Kyra. "She's after the ex. I'm after something else."

"Makes sense." Mike drew in a breath and released it. "All of this sounds easy enough. What type of payment are we talking about?"

"What do you want to be paid?" Kyra asked.

Mike's dark eyes narrowed. "No one asks what I'd like."

"We are." Dubhan waited for the human to come up with a figure.

It didn't take Mike long. "Two grand."

"Five hundred," Kyra countered.

The human shook his head, smiling. "Fifteen hundred."

Kyra blew out a breath and leaned back, pausing. Then she said, "A thousand."

"Deal," Mike stated and held out his hand.

After they'd shook, Mike put his hand out in front of Dubhan. Instead of shaking it, Dubhan said, "We've not come to terms."

The youth blinked, his hand falling to the table. "What?"

"You and Kyra agreed on what she would pay you to look for her ex. I also need information, and I'm willing to pay for it."

Mike shook his head, suddenly wary. "There's a catch."

"No catch," Dubhan assured him. "You want the money or not?"

"I'll get you what you want, but for the thousand that was agreed upon."

Dubhan smiled and held out his hand. "Deal."

They shook just as the food was brought out. The rest of the meal was spent listening to Mike talk about his plans for the future, part of which was opening his own barbershop. It seemed he had a talent with scissors, and that's how he made most of his money.

When the meal was done, Mike said, "I'm guessing you want me to do this today?"

"It would be nice," Dubhan said.

Kyra quickly added, "You could go into the bookstore to look for books on how to start your own business."

"Hmm. That's not a bad idea," Mike said.

Dubhan paid for the meal as Kyra gave Mike the address as well as some spending money and told him to meet them back at the café in an hour. The mortal agreed and walked out.

"I told you that you'd like him," Kyra said with a smile.

Dubhan chuckled. "He's certainly a character."

She licked her lips, the grin gone. "He could be walking into danger. These are the Others. Or at a minimum, those associated with them."

"Chances are, he knows exactly who owns that bookstore."

"Why didn't you ask him?"

"I want to hear what he has to say when he gets back," Dubhan said. "Mike sits on those steps every day, and while he trims hair, what he really does is observe. You heard him. He can easily pick out the locals from the tourists."

Kyra drummed her fingers on the table. "Good point."

"Let's go."

"Where?" she asked with a frown.

Dubhan held out his hand as he got to his feet. "We might not be able to enter the bookstore, but I sure want to see what Mike is doing."

Kyra jumped up at his words. They joined hands and walked

from the café. It was easy for Dubhan to spot Mike up ahead, but they didn't follow too closely. He pulled Kyra into an alley and waited to make sure no one was around before he raised his veil. Then they returned to the sidewalk and caught up with Mike.

The mortal was stopped a couple of times by people asking about booking a haircut, confirming that part of his story hadn't been a lie. In no time, Mike reached the bookstore. He pulled out his phone and started the video as he strode up to the door, but right before his hand touched the knob, he paused for just a second. It was enough that both Dubhan and Kyra noticed.

"What was that?" she whispered.

Dubhan lifted a shoulder in a shrug as Mike opened the door and entered.

"I'd love to be in there."

Dubhan agreed. It was hard to wait outside and imagine what might be said or was being done in the bookstore. Minutes passed. Kyra got antsy, shifting her feet and clenching and flexing the fingers of her other hand.

"It'll be fine," hc assured her in a whisper.

She shot him a dark look. "You don't know that."

"He's searching for a book. That takes time."

"That's true," she conceded begrudgingly.

Dubhan hid his smile. For all of Kyra's happy outlook on life, she was the least patient person he knew. Odd how she had two such differing qualities. He'd learned patience before anything else. Maybe that's why it came so easily to him.

Another twenty minutes passed before Mike exited the book-store with a bag in hand. Dubhan noticed the mortal no longer had his phone out.

"He better have gotten a shot of that entire bookstore," Kyra mumbled.

Dubhan was thinking the same thing as they followed Mike to the café. This time, his steps were quicker, his stride longer as if he were in a hurry. They let Mike enter the restaurant first. Dubhan made Kyra wait another five minutes in an alley before he dropped the veil and they went to meet with Mike.

CHAPTER
fourteen

Kyra was nervous. She hated the emotion. It sent her mind and body in all sorts of directions except the one she needed—calm.

If she and Dubhan couldn't find Xaneth, she hoped they could at least find out something on the Others. Since her life was now on the line, she had a stake in things. Because of that, she didn't want to ask Dubhan if he could help her find out anything about Eva. But it was her aunt. Eva had done so much for her. The least Kyra could do was ask Dubhan if he could discover anything.

When she and Dubhan approached the table where Mike sat, the mortal appeared at ease. That could mean that nothing untoward had happened to him while he was in the shop, or it could mean that he knew exactly who was in the store and hadn't been worried about being caught since he was also part of those associated with the Others.

Dubhan waited for her to sit before he sank into a chair. Mike stared at them, but no one spoke other than to place orders for coffee.

Finally, Dubhan asked, "Well?"

"It's a small bookstore," Mike said. "Very narrow, with piles and piles of books. I thought the library had a lot, but this shop has so many, there's no way anyone could find what they want without the help of those who work there."

"What does that have to do with anything?" she asked.

Mike added sugar and cream to his coffee and stirred it, tapping the spoon on the side before setting it on a napkin. Then he took a sip and set the cup down. "It means that I had a look around while filming as much as I could before it became apparent that there was no real order to the merchandise. At least not like other bookstores I've been in."

"In other words, you had to ask for help," Dubhan said.

Mike nodded. "Precisely. And I couldn't exactly have my phone out for all of that. I did the best I could, but I wanted both of you to know that I couldn't get it all."

Kyra scooted to the end of the chair. "What did you get?"

"Enough, I hope. If not, I'll go back," he offered as he pulled out his mobile phone and laid it on the table. Then he hit play.

Kyra and Dubhan stared transfixed at the small screen as they watched the recording of Mike entering the store. It was as narrow and jumbled with books as he said. Most of the volumes weren't standing up on shelves, but rather on their sides or stacked on the floor.

Mike walked the entire length and width of the store, catching almost all of it. Kyra wasn't sure there was anything to see since it was all just books, books, and more books. She had to agree with Mike, she'd never seen so many in one small place before.

"Rewind," Dubhan ordered.

Mike reached out and began to move the mark on the screen backwards. "How far."

Dubhan's gaze was narrowed. "There."

Kyra leaned forward for a better view to try and see if she could see what had captured Dubhan's attention. They ended up watching it three times, and on the last one, she saw it—the same symbol on the door was carved into one of the bookshelves.

They finished watching the video and heard a part of the conversation when a young woman near Mike's age approached him. She led him to the section of books he was looking for, and then she helped him sort through them. It wasn't until she handed him a volume that Mike put his phone away. The audio was still on, so they heard everything until he left the shop.

"What do you think?" Mike asked when it was done.

Dubhan jerked his chin to the phone. "Rewind to the part we watched several times. Can you enlarge the books in that case?"

"Sure," Mike said and did as requested.

Kyra didn't know what she expected the books to be about, but it certainly wasn't paranormal romance.

Dubhan took the mobile phone and watched the entire video again, stopping and starting it, enlarging in places, and looking at every detail. During this, Kyra kept Mike busy.

"There was no man in the shop," she said.

Mike shook his head sadly. "I'm sorry. I really wanted to help you."

"You have. This lead could be nothing."

"For you. Obviously, he found what he wanted," Mike said with a grin as he nodded toward Dubhan.

Kyra laughed softly. "Tell me, what kind of vibe did you get from the store?"

"Vibe?" Mike gave her a skeptical look. "Are you some New Age people or something?"

"Depends on how you define New Age," she replied with a flash of a smile. "In truth, I've always believed that everything gives off energy. Plants, animals, the ground, and most especially, people. You've run across those you knew not to approach, right?"

Mike shrugged, nodding his head. "Yeah, I suppose."

"That's someone who doesn't want anyone bothering him. He gives off those negative vibes to keep others away. Although, there are some who don't even realize they're giving off such energy. Then there are those who you encounter that can turn your bad day good because of their positive energy that they share with others around them. And last but not least, you have those who suck the energy right out of you. Some do it on purpose, but people don't even realize they're doing it."

Mike's forehead was furrowed as he contemplated her words. "I've never thought of things that way, but you're right."

"So, knowing all of that, what was the energy like in the bookstore?"

"Calm," he replied immediately. "It was peaceful. I wanted to stay longer, but when I noticed the time, I knew I should leave and report to both of you."

Kyra didn't say that it was probably some form of magic used. If those mortals were with the Others, then that meant they were likely Druids. While she knew there were a handful of Druids on the realm with enough magic to stand their ground with the Fae, for the most part, none of them were strong enough to take on one of the Fae.

"It was also clean."

She raised her brows at his words. "That's important?"

"There was no dust on the books. That means someone is cleaning regularly, right?"

"It would appear so." Again, most likely magic.

Kyra glanced at Dubhan, but he was still enthralled with the video. It sucked not being able to watch it and comment with him, but that would have to happen later.

"Here is the rest of your money," Kyra said and slid the folded bills across the table under a napkin. She had added an extra thousand to it, to give Mike the two grand he'd originally asked for.

Mike lifted the napkin and looked at the bills. "That's too much."

"You deserve every penny," Dubhan said without looking up from the mobile screen.

Mike's gaze moved from Dubhan to her. "There is more going on here, isn't there?"

"There is always more to every story," she answered.

The youth snorted and shook his head. "It's okay. It's probably better that I don't know. If either of you needs anything again, I'm willing to help."

Kyra smiled at the mortal. "We'll definitely keep you in mind."

Dubhan handed the mobile back to Mike. "Thank you."

Kyra got to her feet. As she was turning away, she spotted the bag from the bookstore. She stopped and asked, "What books did you buy?"

"Two on how to start a business," Mike said. "Then the girl suggested I try a fiction novel."

Kyra shared a look with Dubhan before she asked Mike, "Do you mind if I look at the books?"

The mortal shook his head and passed her the bag. Kyra pulled out the two business books and handed them to Dubhan to look over. Then she withdrew a fantasy book with dragons on the cover. That wasn't so out of the ordinary since many books in that genre had dragons in them. But it was the girl on the front with red eyes and silver in her black hair, holding an iridescent orb of magic between her hands that caught Kyra's eye.

Without a doubt, the female was a Dark Fae.

Kyra showed it to Dubhan and looked at Mike. "Do you often read fantasy?"

"I'm not much into fiction. I don't even watch a lot of television," he explained. "I like to keep my feet firmly rooted in reality."

Kyra laughed, a feeling of unease running through her. "Do you think there was any particular reason the girl showed you this book?"

Dubhan handed the novel to Mike while the mortal smiled. "I have no idea. I only bought it because I was hoping it would give me a chance to ask her out later."

"Be careful," Dubhan told Mike. "And if you need anything, simply say my name or Kyra's."

Mike jerked his head back, his face scrunching into folds of confusion. "Don't you guys have a mobile?"

Kyra used her magic to make a cell appear. She pulled it out of her pocket and waved it at Mike. "Dubhan likes to tease people." She gave him the number. "And send the video to me, please."

"Doing it now," Mike said.

They waved and walked out. When they were out of the shop, Kyra said, "I can't believe you told him to just say our names. He already thinks we're weird."

"I bet he knows exactly what you are."

She glanced at Dubhan and shook her head. "I don't think so."

"You didn't see him look at you earlier. He knows you're Fae, but he doesn't want to say it."

"It doesn't really matter. I'm just glad he helped us. Did you see anything on the video?"

Dubhan maneuvered her into an alley before teleporting them to her cottage. "I only saw the symbol once, but it seemed out of place there. I heard and saw only the one girl working."

"But you think there were others?"

"I do."

Kyra's mobile dinged, and she looked down to see a text from Mike with the video. "I have a feeling the girl knew exactly what Mike was doing."

"If that's the case, she had him purchase the fiction book on purpose. Maybe to show us she knows what we're doing."

Kyra thought about that for a moment. "I honestly don't think Mike is working with or for the Others, but something is off."

"How so?"

She shrugged, unable to find the words. "Mike said and did all the right things. He taped the entire visit at the store, even giving us audio when he couldn't video it."

"But?" Dubhan pressed.

"He could be lying."

"The mortal isn't lying."

Dubhan's eyes widened at the sound of the voice. Kyra whirled around and found a man and woman standing behind her. The man was tall with thick, black hair and deep purple eyes. He stared at her as if unsure of what he thought of her.

The woman was petite and so stunningly beautiful that Kyra was taken aback. The woman's long, wavy, blue-black hair was braided on one side by her right ear before falling free with the rest of her locks. And her lavender eyes were locked on Kyra.

"I didn't know you were coming," Dubhan said to them.

Kyra couldn't look away from the woman. There was something commanding and powerful about her. Kyra wasn't exactly frightened, but she wasn't at ease either.

"We've been following both of you all morning," the male said.

The woman stepped forward. "My name is Erith, though you might know me better as Death."

The room began to spin as Kyra tried to remain standing.

All she could think was is this what it feels like to die.

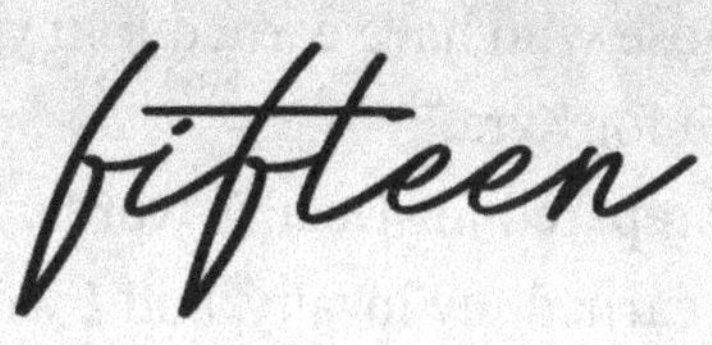

CHAPTER
fifteen

For the first time, Dubhan felt fear. It gripped him tightly, squeezing the air from his lungs—and common sense from his brain.

"Following us?" Dubhan questioned.

Cael's purple gaze locked on him, daring him to question Death further. Dubhan had to actually clench his teeth to stop the words he yearned to speak. Being a Reaper meant never questioning Erith.

This was the first time Dubhan had ever done such a thing. He didn't regret it, though. He might serve Death, but he wouldn't stand by while Cael killed Kyra simply because she had been smart enough to figure out he was a Reaper.

"I see our presence has upset both of you," Erith stated calmly. She gave Kyra a smile. "There's no need to be frightened of me."

"I beg to differ," Kyra said, her voice shaking. "You're Death."

Dubhan moved to stand beside Kyra. He didn't say anything as his and Cael's gazes remained locked.

It was Death who blew out a breath. "Dubhan, I knew the moment you looked into my eyes and accepted my offer to join the Reapers that you would always remain loyal. For you give such allegiance only to those who have earned it in your eyes. I see that same devotion in you for Kyra."

Dubhan wasn't prepared for Death's words. He looked into her lavender eyes. "You earned my loyalty, and I will always be one of your Reapers."

"But?" Erith urged when he grew quiet.

"Kyra deserves to live," he said. "She got caught up in magic, was in the wrong place at the wrong time, and it was her intelligence that helped her figure out who we were."

Cael quirked a brow as he asked, "And her ability to find you?"

Dubhan still couldn't quite explain that. "I don't know."

"I do," Erith said as her eyes moved to Kyra.

Kyra shifted nervously. "It's not a spell. I swear. I just kept thinking about him, and the next thing I knew, he was there."

"I know." Death's lips curved into a grin. "You are one of the Kavanaughs, Kyra. You can take away the pain of others, which is a rare gift in itself. That is how I know you didn't use a spell to find Dubhan."

Dubhan looked from Erith to Kyra, thoroughly confused. "What?"

"We followed you today, remember?" Cael asked. "During that time, we did a little investigating of our own and discovered Kyra was from the ancient Kavanaugh line. The original one."

Death nodded. "Which is how I realized how Kyra found you."

"Wait. Ancient? Original?" Kyra asked, dumbstruck. "You must be mistaken. My family line isn't that old."

Cael chuckled as he shook his head. "Actually, it's one of the oldest Fae families. There are thirty books from each of the ancient lines, but the Kavanaughs go back even further. Your family is one of the founding five."

Dubhan wasn't sure who was more shocked, him or Kyra. He'd known she was special, but he hadn't realized just how much. "Why does that matter?"

"Because every few generations there is one gifted with a special power," Erith explained. Her gaze returned to Kyra. "Those who have this unusual ability are able to locate their other half, but only after meeting them."

Silence filled the room.

Kyra swallowed, the sound loud in the stillness. She didn't look Dubhan's way, and he tried not to be offended—especially after just learning that the only way she could've found him was if they were soulmates. To say that he was speechless was the understatement of the millennia.

"I never heard anyone in my family speak of this . . . power," Kyra finally said.

Cael shrugged. "From what I understand, few in your family even talk about the ability to take pain from others."

"That's true." Kyra drew in a ragged breath. As she did, her fingers reached out and curled around his.

Dubhan wanted to shout for joy at that simple action. He held her hand firmly, letting her know that he was there, that he would always stand beside her. It surprised him, this sudden emotion.

"We can discuss all of this at a later date," Death said. "Right now, we have more pressing issues."

Cael crossed his arms over his chest, distaste filling his face. "The Others."

Dubhan cleared his throat. "You said Mike told us the truth."

"He did, but he wasn't the only one involved in all of this," Erith said.

Kyra frowned as she glanced at Dubhan. "I didn't lie. And if Dubhan, I, nor Mike lied, then who did?"

"The girl in the bookstore," Erith answered.

"But . . . how did you enter? It's warded against Fae."

Dubhan turned his head to Kyra and said, "Erith is a goddess. While she does pass judgment on the Fae, she isn't one of us."

Kyra's eyes widened as they swung to Death. "Oh. I see."

"What was the girl lying about?" Dubhan asked.

Erith lifted one shoulder in a shrug. "That human is a Druid, which you already figured out. Her family was one of the original mies to join the Others."

Kyra's gaze moved to the side, her brow furrowed. "I still have yet to understand why the mies would join the Others. The droughs it's easy to understand. Those Druids who gave themselves to evil and all the power that came with it."

"I don't care why they did it," Cael said in a tone edged with the barest hint of anger. "I just want them to leave this realm and never return."

Dubhan ran a hand over his mouth and jaw. "You said the female was lying to Mike. Do you think she knew we sent him?"

"Yes," Erith replied with a single nod.

Kyra asked, "How do you know that?"

"I just do." Death looked at Cael a moment before her gaze slid to Dubhan. "I believe Mike will be safe, but the Others—or at least those who wish to be with the Others or are associated with them —now have both of you on their radar. They don't know you're a Reaper, but that could change."

Dubhan wasn't afraid of some group. He'd always been willing and eager for battle. It was the only thing he'd known for most of his life. It wasn't until the Reapers that he learned what a true family was, and even then, not until Eoghan had taken over as leader.

Dubhan had siblings, but he didn't think of them as family. His fellow Reapers and Death, they were his family. He learned to trust and be trustworthy from them.

"The Others have their sights set on the Dragon Kings," Death continued. "But I have a feeling if they discover the Reapers, then they will come after us."

"And both of you," Dubhan said, nodding his head to her and Cael. "You're a goddess, and Cael is now a god."

Kyra's mouth fell open in surprise. "If both of you have such power, why not just get rid of the Others now?"

"This realm is the Dragon Kings' domain. They have guarded it and defended it numerous times." Death drew in a breath and then slowly released it. "They made the decision to allow the humans to live here, and it cost them everything. But even then, it didn't diminish the Kings. If anything, it made them stronger. The Others believe they've weakened the Dragon Kings."

Cael dropped his arms to his sides. "Perhaps they have."

Erith shook her head, smiling. "No." Then her lavender eyes moved to Kyra. "It isn't my duty or Cael's to take down the Others. But more than that, I have faith in the Kings to stand against the Others on their own and fight them."

"There isn't a Fae alive who doesn't know and respect the Dragon Kings. They are immensely powerful, and I'm sure they can take down the Others themselves, but should they? If you judge the Fae, and the Fae are part of the Others, why aren't the Reapers involved?" Kyra asked.

Dubhan didn't even hide his smile. He happened to agree with Kyra. And he loved that she wasn't afraid to speak her mind in front of Death.

It was Cael who said, "I don't disagree with you, Kyra, but there are more to the Others than you know. And I'm not sure we're only dealing with the Others here. The humans didn't just arrive on this realm one day. They were brought by a group of Druids from another realm."

"I'm not sure how that changes things," she said and looked at Dubhan for a moment. "If this realm is home to the Fae because the Kings allowed it, and some of those same Fae have joined forces with others to take down the Dragon Kings—as the Others or not—don't those of us who know now have an obligation to stand with the Kings against them? I know I will, regardless of what anyone else does. Because to do nothing is akin to siding with the Others against the very beings who share this incredible realm with us."

Dubhan couldn't take his eyes from Kyra. He had never been able to put his thoughts and feelings into words, but she had done it with ease—and without any condemnation.

"I like her," Cael said.

Dubhan faced Kyra. "You would stand with the Dragon Kings against your own?"

"If there are those who want to take down the beings who are honorable and good simply because they are powerful, then . . . absolutely," Kyra answered.

Dubhan then looked from Cael to Erith. "I serve you. I will always serve you, and I will always follow your commands. However, Kyra made an excellent point. The Others were created because they feared the Dragon Kings. What will they do when they learn of us? Or you?"

"They wouldn't live a second longer," Erith stated, anger burning in her eyes.

Cael sighed and turned his head to Death. "I know why we've

stayed out of things. We weren't needed in the latest battle against Usaeil, but this is different."

"You would have us join the Kings?" Erith asked him. "All of us?"

Dubhan quickly interjected, "No. I would use our skills to everyone's advantage."

Death's gaze narrowed on him for a moment before she smiled. "Now that is something I hadn't considered. We can stay hidden until we're needed."

"Not until we're needed," Cael said. "We remain hidden to get the advantage."

Dubhan grinned, his excitement growing. "Like coming up behind them."

"Oh, that's good," Kyra said to him.

They shared a quick smile.

Death, however, didn't seem convinced. "We have no idea how long it'll be before the battle comes."

"It'll be quicker than you think," Cael said.

Her lips twisted. "You're probably right. Now that Usaeil has been defeated, the Kings can focus solely on the Others."

"That's not all they have to worry about," Cael said cryptically.

Dubhan had no idea what Cael was speaking of, but Dubhan wasn't worried. The Dragon Kings were the ultimate warriors. He'd seen them fighting together during the Fae Wars. He'd been terrified of them—and with good reason.

"What about Rhi?" Kyra said.

Dubhan's gaze immediately went to Erith, but she didn't look his way. In fact, she kept her eyes lowered.

"That's . . . a difficult situation," Cael finally answered.

Kyra snorted. "It's not. Rhi is one of the best fighters we have. She's still out there, and we're going to need her."

Cael grinned at Kyra. "You certainly don't hesitate to speak your mind."

"I say what needs to be said."

Dubhan lifted her hand to his lips and kissed it. "First, we need to deal with those coming after you."

"After us," she corrected.

He conceded that. "Us."

"That's why we're here," Erith said. "I might have thought to let the Kings deal with the Others themselves, but there is no way I'll allow that group anywhere near my Reapers. Or those they've chosen. I had another mission for you, Dubhan, but I think you and Kyra need to stay on your present course."

Dubhan bowed his head at Death because he knew she had just given her blessing for him and Kyra to be together. Which was a good thing, because he wasn't sure what he would've done had she not. That's how much he loved Kyra.

Not even thinking that frightened him. Because Kyra gave him the courage to hold onto things he hadn't believed he was good enough for.

CHAPTER

sixteen

'm a little gobsmacked," Kyra said when she was alone with Dubhan once more.

He cocked a brow. "You didn't appear it."

She looked around. "Are they really gone?"

"I don't know," he said with a shrug of his broad shoulders. "They could still be here."

Kyra blew out a breath. "Holy smokes. I just spoke with Death."

Dubhan's lips curved into a smile.

She laughed and faced him. "Death. I actually spoke with Death. And she's gorgeous. I didn't know a creature could be so stunning. How were you not falling all over yourself to get her into your bed?"

"She's beautiful, yes, but she's not my type."

"Now, that's the perfect answer."

Dubhan dragged her to him and wrapped his arms around her.

"You've not said anything about what Erith told us regarding how you found me."

"I haven't really had much time to think about it."

"And now?"

She chuckled. "You don't give a girl much time, do you?"

"I want to know your thoughts."

She ran her hands over his chest as she looked at the collar of his shirt. "I think I knew in the back of my mind that in order for me to find you the way I did, it had to be for a special reason."

Her gaze lifted to meet his crimson orbs. "It was like a switch flipped inside me when I saw you fighting those Trackers. I couldn't take my eyes from you."

"You didn't know me," he said softly.

She brushed her fingers over the hard edge of his jaw. "My soul did. It's the only way I can explain it. I recognized you, and I could think of nothing else but getting close to you."

"I can't tell you how glad I am that you did find me."

"But," she said, swallowing. "You don't believe in soulmates, do you?"

A small frown furrowed his brow. "I didn't say that."

She gave him a pointed look.

It was his turn to look away. "Up until I became a Reaper, I didn't think love really existed. Then, I saw it firsthand when Eoghan—the one who leads my group—fell in love with Thea. Even then, I believed it was some fluke. It didn't matter that other Reapers had fallen in love. I hadn't seen it. Then, I witnessed Death and Cael finally admitting their love for each other. That love saved both of them." He drew in a breath and looked at her. "I like the person I am when I'm with you. You make me see everything in a different light."

She smiled at his words.

His gaze became heated. "And then there's the fact that I can't keep my hands off you."

"Which I really like, by the way," she interjected.

He gave her a quick kiss. "I don't know much about love, but I know what I feel for you. It's deep and strong, and without a doubt, I know I've fallen for you."

Euphoria burst through Kyra. She threw her arms around Dubhan's neck as their lips met. The kiss he gave her was full of raw hunger and primal longing—and she felt the same inside herself. She hadn't known what to expect by following a Reaper, but she certainly hadn't counted on falling in love or learning more about her family than she'd ever known.

It was Dubhan who ended the kiss. He was breathing loudly, his chest rising and falling quickly as he looked at her. "You're the only thing that could make me forget about my duties or going into battle."

"Really?" she asked with a grin. "I like that I can do that."

"Woman, you do so much more."

"Tell me we'll survive this thing with the Others," she said worriedly.

He smoothed back her hair and looked deep into her eyes. "I give you my vow that, as long as I'm alive, I will fight them with everything I have to keep you safe. Because I love you."

Knowing how he felt and hearing the words were two different things. Warmth spread through her at his declaration. "I love you," she told him.

They stood in silence for a moment before she asked, "What do we do now?"

"I don't know," he replied with a bark of laughter. "I don't like waiting around for my enemies to find me, but at the same time, I don't want to go looking for them with you near either."

"I won't be left behind," she told him.

"I wouldn't dream of it."

She nodded. "As long as we have that cleared up."

"But I won't have you in danger."

His serious tone reminded her of their situation. "Because I don't know how to fight?"

"That is part of it. The fact that you're willing to go into a fight if you have to makes the entire situation volatile. Anything could happen. You could win."

"Or I could lose," she said with a nod. "I know. What is the other part?"

He flattened his lips for a moment. "I can't lose you."

"Now you understand how I feel at the thought of you facing the Others."

Dubhan nodded slowly. "I do, indeed."

Kyra stepped out of his arms and took his hand to lead him to the window to look out over the valley. "Like you, I don't particularly want to wait around for our enemies to find us. We could continue our search for Xaneth."

"He isn't here, and as much as I hoped to be the one to find him, I think that will fall to another of us."

"I took you away from the search." Kyra didn't like that.

He shook his head. "No, you helped me find myself. And you. Not to mention, you said everything I wanted to say about the Others to Death, when I couldn't find the words."

"Even if you had the words, I don't think you would've told her."

"You're probably right, but I think, in the end, I would have. We shouldn't be sitting around watching as the Dragon Kings get hit on all sides by this group."

Kyra turned to face him. "Dubhan, if that symbol on the bookstore actually means the Druids are part of the Others, or even some other group like the Others, then—"

"So is my family most likely." He nodded. "I've accepted that."

"Did you hear or see anything before you were a Reaper that might help?"

He squeezed the bridge of his nose with his thumb and forefinger. "I can't say that I did, but I could have and not realized it. We didn't have visitors at the house. Ever. Not even family came. We went to everyone. I always wondered why that was."

"Do you recall that same mark being on the houses of your other family members?"

Dubhan's gaze went far-off as his thoughts turned to the past. "I can't remember." He gave a shake of his head and returned his gaze to her. "It's enough that my family is involved in such a group."

"You aren't."

"I was. Without even knowing it."

"You can't hold onto those kinds of thoughts. You didn't know any differently."

He snorted and faced the window. "I did. I might not have known what my parents were involved in, but I knew it was something that would make our family stronger in the end. I was fine with that. For a while."

"You chose a different path. Remember that."

"I wouldn't change any of it," he said as he turned his head to her. "All of it made me who I am today. It led me to become a Reaper, which then brought me to you."

"Actually, I found you," she said with a smile.

He grinned and took her hand. "That's right. You did find me."

They turned back to the window in unison as they held hands, each lost in thought. Kyra knew there was a very good chance that

Dubhan would have to fight his family if Death decided that the Reapers would join forces with the Dragon Kings to battle the Others.

Kyra wasn't sure she could do that if the positions were reversed. Then again, she might not get along with her family, but they hadn't betrayed her and killed her either. That would certainly change her thinking.

"We'll join the Kings," Dubhan said into the silence.

Kyra glanced his way. "You think Erith will allow that?"

"Allow?" He flashed a quick grin. "You made her see another side that she hadn't considered. But, yes, I do think she will join with the Kings, and then she will let us make our own decision."

Now that wasn't something Kyra had expected to hear. "Let you make your own decision? I thought you served her and did as she demanded."

Dubhan's face swung toward her. "We do, but this isn't just any battle. This is one that could wipe out an entire race."

"Do the Others actually have that kind of power?"

"Actually, they do."

He pulled her to the couch and tugged her down beside him as he began telling her one tale after another of how the Others had set traps millions of years ago for the Dragon Kings. Kyra was in turns stunned and shaken at the lengths the Others had gone to in order to get what they wanted.

"And Usaeil was part of it?" Kyra asked.

Dubhan nodded slowly. "She was, but despite that, she wanted Con for her own."

"To give the Kings babies?" she asked in disbelief.

"They are unable to have children with mortals."

Kyra wrinkled her nose. "But Usaeil's plan didn't come to fruition. She failed. And now she's dead."

"Is she?"

"Her body is gone. I figured Death took it."

Dubhan didn't say anything.

Kyra looked pointedly at him. "Did she?"

"I don't know every move Erith makes. For all I know, she did indeed take Usaeil's body. I know Death said that Rhi needed to be the one to kill the queen."

"Interesting." Kyra had only met the famed Fae once, but she had instantly liked Rhi. The Light just had that kind of personality.

Dubhan frowned. "What?"

"Nothing. I was just thinking. I wasn't there to see the battle, but I heard enough Fae talking about it. Both the Light and the Dark are in disarray. Neither have leaders, and it's going to take a toll."

"There will be infighting as those eying the thrones try to take them."

Kyra sighed heavily. "One of the many reasons I never liked court. No doubt someone there is already searching for Usaeil's descendent to take the throne."

"That would be Xaneth. Or. . . ."

He trailed off, making Kyra more interested than ever. "I'm guessing you know of another?"

"I do. So did Usaeil, but I think she forgot him in her madness. Or perhaps she didn't think he was a threat. Regardless, I'm pretty sure he doesn't want the throne."

"Which leaves us with Xaneth."

Dubhan made a sound in the back of his throat. "Which will do us no good if we can't find him."

"Would he take over as king?"

"I don't know him well enough to be able to answer that. He's certainly intelligent and shrewd enough to make a good leader."

"But if he doesn't want it, we're right back to square one," Kyra said with a frown.

"The Dark are different."

She winced at the thought. "They've never used bloodlines to determine who will lead. It's always been the strongest, right?"

"It has."

"Anyone come to mind?"

Dubhan slowly shook his head. "I was actually hoping Balladyn would remain king for some time. I liked him."

"His body disappeared as well, from what I hear." Kyra stared at Dubhan, waiting for some sign that would indicate that he knew something, but all she got was a shrug.

Was it coincidence that both Balladyn's and Usaeil's bodies had vanished after their deaths? Did Death take them? And if not, then who did?

And more importantly, why?

CHAPTER

seventeen

Sitting still was something Dubhan had mastered long ago, but that day, he found it impossible to wait. He'd always been a man of action, not someone who bided his time, waiting for things to come to him.

His eyes landed on Kyra, who walked around the cottage. She had come to him, but he hadn't been waiting for her. Or had he?

Ever since Eoghan had fallen in love with Thea, Dubhan had wondered if he was capable of such an emotion. Now, he knew the truth. For someone who hadn't known what love was, he was surprised that he recognized it. Then again, something that profound wasn't easily overlooked.

"I need to keep myself occupied," Kyra said as she came out from her room with an armful of items. This time, her hair bangs were orange, the rest of her locks red, and her eyes green. She halted when she saw him staring. "What?"

"Do you not like your natural coloring?" he asked.

She shrugged. "It's a habit now. I don't even realize I'm doing it half the time. Do you not like it?"

"I like it fine. I also really enjoy your natural hair and eyes."

A heartbeat later, her eyes returned to silver, and her hair to the wavy, black strands that fell to her shoulders.

He smiled at her. "You can wear your hair and eyes any color you want. I will think you're beautiful in all of it."

Kyra was smiling when she joined him on the sofa. "Let's try this out for a bit."

"Sounds good. Now, what were you saying? You need to keep occupied?"

She nodded and placed the items on the coffee table. She opened the map of the world and then set a vial of small pins with colored ends on them near her. There were markers of various colors, as well as pencils, and some sticky tabs.

"Oh," she said and jumped up to go into the kitchen.

Dubhan watched as she opened a bottle of wine and poured two glasses. And all of it had been done without any magic. He found it endearing that she went about life in such a way. He wouldn't have done that, but that's what made her so special.

She looked up and grinned. "Still getting used to me not using magic, huh?"

"Something like that."

"Here," she said and handed him his glass of wine. "There are times when using magic is easier."

"Like all the time?" he asked with a raised brow.

She chuckled before she took a drink. "True, but I like doing things like this."

She might not be a warrior, but she was strong-willed and didn't hesitate to follow her heart. Dubhan hadn't met many women like that. In truth, Aisling had been the first. Well, besides Death.

Aisling might be the only female Reaper, but she was a force to be reckoned with. He'd heard her some nights, gripped in the claws of her nightmares. She trusted no one but her fellow Reapers, and even then, Dubhan suspected that Aisling believed her time could end at any second.

She lived life to the fullest. Everything she did, she did with all her might and passion. There were no half measures with the female. And he'd rarely seen anyone as adept on the battlefield as Aisling.

He'd liked her instantly, even though she kept him at arm's length. She didn't need his protection, but Dubhan couldn't help feeling protective of her. Almost as if she were his younger sister. He'd never told her any of that, and she'd likely give him a black eye for it, but there was no denying that the kinship he felt for Aisling is what helped him trust the other Reapers.

"You're deep in thought."

He blinked and focused on Kyra. "Sorry."

"Don't be," she told him and put a hand on his knee. "You all right?"

"I'm perfect. Show me what you have here."

She smiled excitedly. "Use these pins and show me everywhere you've looked for Xaneth. If you know where others have looked, marked those, as well."

"We keep it all in our heads."

"Humor me," she urged.

Dubhan shrugged and did as she asked. Ten minutes later, he sat back and surveyed the map and the areas that he had searched.

"Is this just your searching? Or the other Reapers, as well?" Kyra asked.

"Mostly mine, but there were occasions when we searched in teams. I added what I knew. What is this?"

Kyra sat back, her knees pulled to her chest as she stared at the map. "I don't know, exactly. I just had the urge to get out the map and find the locations you had been to."

"Kinda like how you had to look for me?" he asked.

She glanced at him, nodding.

"Then don't stop," he told her. "I'll ask the other Reapers to add in their locations."

"Could you?"

Dubhan might not fully understand how Kyra's mind worked, but he didn't need to. Whatever power or magic had given her the ability to find him, might also do the same to locate Xaneth somehow.

"Don't worry," she told him with a grin. "I don't have romantic feelings for Xaneth."

Dubhan wrapped his arm around her and pulled her against him. "I'm not the jealous type. Or at least I've not had reason to be in the past." He frowned. "Hmm. Maybe I am jealous."

Kyra laughed and looked up at him. "We will get through this."

"Yes, we will." He sat up, forcing her up, as well. "We need to talk about what to do if the Others appear."

"Okay. What do you want me to do?"

"Get out of here. Teleport somewhere safe."

She was shaking her head before he'd even finished. "I'm not leaving."

"Not to be indelicate, but you aren't a fighter."

"I'm aware," she said with a smile. "But I'm not running away this time."

"I can't even tell you to stay near me because the moment they realize the depths of my power, they'll come at me with everything they have."

Kyra cocked a brow. "So?"

He looked at her a moment. "What do you mean?"

"You're a bloody Reaper."

"Did you not hear the stories I told you earlier? The Dragon Kings have the greatest magic of any beings on this realm. And for all I know, the greatest of any realm. Light and Dark Fae, and mie and drough Druids, joined their magic together to create something so strong that it can set the Kings back on their arses."

She didn't seem fazed by his words. "You aren't a Dragon King."

"I'm aware."

With a roll of her eyes, she replied, "My point is that you said Death gave you some of her power to become a Reaper. She returned your soul to you, increased your magic, and enhanced your senses. Right?"

He nodded.

"Well, if she isn't afraid of the Others, why should you be? My guess is that their magic won't affect any of the Reapers or Death and Cael like it will the Kings."

At this he frowned. "Why do you say that? The Kings' magic is greater than even a Reaper's."

"And Death's?" she asked.

Dubhan shrugged. "I honestly have no idea. Erith has incredible power, but then so do the Dragon Kings."

"And you think because the Kings are affected by the Others' magic, that all of you will be, as well?"

He gave her a pointed look. "It stands to reason, yes."

"Hmm," she said and looked away, lost in thought.

Dubhan waited as she continued looking at something in the

distance. The Reapers had been so focused on first Bran and then finding Xaneth that none of them had stopped to think about the Others.

Or what might happen if they defeated the Dragon Kings.

Dubhan knew it was a long shot to think the Kings might lose, but it was a scenario that had to be considered. He couldn't figure out why it was so important to the Druids to defeat the Kings.

The Dragon Kings hadn't gone exploring other realms. They were content with their home. Yet they had made room for the mortals and Fae—and look what that had brought the Kings.

"Have any of the Kings been unaffected by the Others' magic?" Kyra asked suddenly.

Dubhan thought for a moment. "Unaffected is probably the wrong word. V was able to find a weakness in their magic and eventually break it apart, but it took him some time."

"All the Kings need to know how to do that. And so do the Reapers."

"That's not a bad idea," he said.

Kyra licked her lips. "There's also something else to consider."

"What's that?"

"Do exactly what the Others have done. Combine your magic."

He blinked, his mind going blank at the suggestion. His first impulse was to refuse, but then a moment later, he reconsidered it.

"Exactly," Kyra said. "If the Others' magic, which is nothing more than Fae and Druid combined, can hinder a Dragon King, can you imagine what magic from the Kings and Reapers could do?"

"It would be more powerful."

She nodded.

Dubhan leaned back and blew out a breath. "The Others use

their magic in traps and situations where the Kings aren't prepared. Not once have the Kings faced the Others head-on."

"And you don't think they ever will?"

"I don't know," he replied honestly. "It stands to reason that the Others have always known exactly what course the Kings will take and set things directly in their path to thwart them. Why would they gather and stand for a fight when they don't have to?"

"But they do."

Dubhan shook his head. "They don't. For all we know, they've set thousands more traps that will eventually take out the Kings one by one. Look what they did to V, taking his memories for those eons of time."

"I disagree," Kyra said. "If the Others didn't intend to make a stand, they wouldn't have put up symbols to announce who they are. They don't need to let members of their group know who they are. They did it to alert anyone who might be looking for them."

Shite. She was right. Dubhan ran a hand through his hair. "Erith said the girl in the bookshop knew we'd sent Mike in. She gave him that fantasy book for a reason. I wonder if we weren't meant to read it, as well?"

Kyra shrugged and raised her brows. "I think we should find out. More than that, I think we should let the others know all of this."

"I hope you're wrong."

"Me, too. Otherwise, we need to prepare for war sooner rather than later."

Dubhan briefly closed his eyes. "And with the Light and Dark in disarray without leaders, they're primed for someone to step in and take over."

"You don't think the Others would do that, do you?"

"I think the Fae involved in the Others would."

Kyra's mouth formed an O.

Dubhan got to his feet as he called for Death.

CHAPTER

Somewhere . . .

He missed the sun. Xaneth looked up at the semi-dark sky and cringed. Nothing changed in this world Usaeil had put him in. The sky was a peculiar blue color that bordered on purple and stuck in perpetual dusk. No moon. No sun.

That was enough to drive someone insane. But Xaneth wouldn't let himself get that far. Although, he wasn't sure what he could do.

He'd been running from the creature after him for . . . well, he wasn't sure how long he'd been in this hellhole, but it felt like an eternity. The beast always seemed to find him. Xaneth couldn't rest for any length of time. He had to stay on the move, had to stay as hidden as he could just so he could remain alive.

It had been some time since he'd heard his aunt's voice coming down from the sky like she was some god. How he hated Usaeil.

He hoped that someone—Death, Rhi, the Dragon Kings, hell, even Balladyn—would kill Usaeil. She was a cancer that needed to be cut out before she infected all Fae.

But he couldn't think about his aunt. She was a nuisance to be sure, but first and foremost, he had to remain alive. At first, he'd thought Usaeil had put him in this place for the creature to kill him, and that might still be what would happen. But he was beginning to suspect that she just wanted to torture him.

What if he quit playing this game of hers? What if he stopped running? What's the worst that could happen? He'd die?

At least he would no longer be in this putrid place of never-ending torment. He didn't fear death. Over the last weeks, he'd actually come to pray for it a few times. Then he'd come to his senses and kept fighting.

But he was growing weary of it all. There was a way out, of that, he was positive. He just had to find it. And if he no longer had the fekking beast running him down, then he might be able to locate it and get back to Earth.

Xaneth squeezed his eyes shut. The growl of the creature was closer now. Xaneth put his hand on the tree, felt the bark digging into his palm. Whatever this place was, it prevented him from using his magic. That didn't deter him, though. He would get out.

There was something that kept niggling at the back of his mind, something he should know, but he couldn't put his finger on what. Every time he tried to concentrate, the thought retreated and got farther and farther away. It was only when he was thinking of something else that it came close enough to tease him with its presence.

Xaneth jumped up from his hiding place behind a giant oak and ran over the rugged terrain, jumping over fallen trees, and using his hands for balance when he slid down steep valleys. He could put enough distance between the creature and himself to allow him the time he needed to climb up the mountains. Some were harder than others, but he always managed to get to the top before the beast appeared.

He slid to a stop, his arms flailing when he came to the edge of a cliff. The dense tree line had hidden the cliff. He glanced over his shoulder, determining how close the beast was. Then he looked over the side of the cliff to see a river below him, jagged rocks protruding from the water, no doubt with many more below the surface.

There was no time for him to retrace his steps and find another route. He only had one choice—jump.

Xaneth didn't hesitate to leap from the edge. For a second, there was silence, and then the whoosh of air rushing past his ears as he plummeted toward the water far below. It felt like forever before he got close enough to the river that he held his breath.

Then he was beneath the water, his senses buffeted by the roar of the currents and the chilly temperature that was so at odds with the warm weather. Xaneth wasn't able to brace himself before he was slammed against a boulder. He did manage to turn himself and use his foot to prevent his body from being hit a second time, though. After that, it was a matter of using the currents and the rocks to rise to the surface.

Once his head was above water, he drew in a deep breath and made himself relax as he floated with the swift current. To fight it would only tire him, and he was already drained. Thankfully, it wasn't long before the rocks disappeared, and the water calmed enough that he was able to swim to shore. His fingers dug into the wet sand as he pulled himself out of the water.

He shivered as the air brushed past him. Xaneth paused to look around. There was something about this place that looked familiar, but he'd never been here before. At least now, he might have more time to get some rest and eat more than the berries he found as he ran through the woods.

Xaneth longed for a fire, but he had no idea how to make one without magic. He'd have to settle for removing his clothes and allowing them to dry. After he'd spread them out on the rocks, he waded barefoot back into the water. Once long, long ago, his father had taken him to a river where he'd tried to teach Xaneth how to catch a fish using his bare hands. Xaneth hadn't been interested at the time. He wanted to swim, not fish, but he still remembered the lesson.

The longer Xaneth stood in the water, the warmer it became. Or maybe he was simply getting used to it. His lower arms and legs were much warmer than the rest of him that wasn't submerged, but that was just one more contradiction in this place Usaeil had thrown him.

The first brush of the fish against his arm made his heart leap. He didn't move, though. The fish got closer and closer, finally swimming between his hands. That's when Xaneth grabbed it and brought it out of the water.

His arms were raised above his head, a smile on his lips as he turned toward the shore. And just like that, the memory was there of him doing this same thing all those years ago, turning to show his father that he'd succeeded.

The breath was sucked out of Xaneth as he got lost in the memory for several seconds. It was the fish wiggling in his hand that pulled him back to the present. Xaneth killed the fish and walked to shore.

He stood with his back to the water, his eyes closed as he recalled as much detail of that day with his father as he could.

Then he turned to the river and opened his eyes. That's when he knew. He wasn't on another realm.

He was locked in his own mind.

Xaneth looked down at his feet and spotted the rock with the sharp edge. He picked it up and used it to clean the fish. He found a smooth boulder and used it for a seat as he ate the raw fish, his mind sorting through what he'd learned.

Usaeil must have used some powerful magic to lock him inside his own head, but that didn't mean he was stuck here forever. He could get out. The problem was . . . how? In many ways, it was more difficult than finding his way off a realm.

"Damn you, Usaeil," he muttered.

But he couldn't allow himself to get bogged down by his hate. He had to get past that in order to clear his mind and discover the exit.

First, he needed to get rid of the creature hounding him. The best way to do that was to lay a trap. Xaneth had been young when he and his father came to the river, that was why he hadn't remembered it at first, nor did he recall the territory around it.

He left his clothes and scouted the area on first one side of the river and then the other. By the time he returned, his clothes were dry, and he put them back on. The fact that considerable time had passed without the beast appearing meant that he had drifted quite a ways on the water.

But how much longer did he have before the creature returned? It wasn't enough for him to set the trap now, but he'd found a location. All he had to do was come up with a way to trap the beast and kill it.

He wanted to stay ahead of the fiend, so he started walking along the river. Now that he didn't have to run, he was able to get a better lay of the land and come up with a design for the trap. The mountain and boulders would help, but it would all come down to the beast following him.

How to kill it was the next question? He couldn't use magic, nor did he have any weapons. Xaneth grinned. There were rocks aplenty, and if he had to bash the beast's head in, he would.

Xaneth kept the river to his left. He went most of the day without hearing the creature, and he used every second of that time to gather the items he needed to make the trap, creating sections of it as he walked, and setting them aside when they were finished. He knew exactly where each part was so he could gather them and take them to the place he'd set to snare the beast.

Since it seemed as if the creature followed his every footstep, Xaneth zigzagged through the woods, making sure to keep under cover as best he could.

Just when he thought he might have lost the beast for good, he heard the growl. Xaneth finished making the last part of the cage and tied off the thick vine that held the sticks together.

He hesitated, wondering if there was enough time for him to circle back around to gather the sections and head to the spot in order to trap the beast, but the second growl was closer. Very close.

Xaneth hid the piece and took off running. He'd rested most of the afternoon, but his walking days seemed to be over. He'd enjoyed it while it lasted, and he was going to make sure that what hunted him didn't last much longer. Because the hunted was about to become the hunter.

nineteen

The silence after Dubhan had told Erith and Cael about her proposal was frightening. Kyra forced herself not to shift her feet or fiddle with her hands. She had spoken her mind to Death earlier. This was no different.

Oh, but it was, and she knew it. Kyra drew in a shaky breath. Erith might have accepted her, but that could be snatched away at any moment.

"I'm actually upset that I didn't think of that sooner," Cael said.

Erith cut him a look before her gaze moved to Kyra. "For someone who hasn't seen battle, you are awfully willing to join it."

"I'm willing because I know what's at stake. Also, they're after me. So, really, I'm just trying to survive," Kyra said.

And why did she have to sound so . . . idiotic? Kyra inwardly rolled her eyes at herself. If only she could sound as impressive as she had earlier. Then again, pressure had a way of causing her to do irrational things.

"I admit, you might have stumbled across a solution," Death said.

Kyra bit back her smile. It wasn't nearly time to celebrate yet. "It just seemed logical."

"Sometimes, others who aren't warriors are what we need because we don't see the entire picture," Dubhan said.

Without looking Dubhan's way, Erith said, "Cael does."

"I have to meditate on it," Cael replied.

Dubhan's forehead furrowed. "You see all?"

Cael shrugged. "If I meditate long enough, I can see the best outcome for a battle."

"That's why you never lost," Dubhan said with a grin.

Cael's smile was his only answer.

Kyra looked between them, trying to read between the lines.

"Did you use that same scenario against Bran?" Dubhan asked.

Cael's smile vanished. "Some things are out of my control."

"The battle with the Others will be, as well," Erith stated. "For all of us. Including the Dragon Kings."

Kyra almost asked if that meant that Death and the Reapers were going to join in, but she thought it best to keep Erith's attention off her for the time being.

In the next heartbeat, Death's lavender eyes swung to her. "The Kings might have made some enemies because of their power, but they've made many more allies. Several of the Kings have mated Druids, some with ties to the Isle of Skye."

Kyra shrugged. "Are the Skye Druids special?"

"Very," Cael answered. "They're the strongest. Every once in a while, a powerful Druid is born outside of Skye. Eilish is one of those. In fact, I would hazard to guess that she's stronger than any Druid on Skye. And she happens to be mated to Ulrik, King of Silvers."

Kyra could hardly believe her ears. "That's good news, then. And I do know of one Fae mated to a King."

"Shara," Dubhan said.

Kyra didn't know why she had a sudden spike of jealousy, but it was there nonetheless. Maybe it was the way Dubhan had said her name. Or perhaps Kyra was reading too much into it. But everyone knew of the Dark Fae who had become Light and mated a Dragon King. Shara was a legend, especially because so many Light had been told that no Dark could return to the Light. But since it was Usaeil who had told them that, it had obviously been a lie.

"Did you know her?" Cael asked Dubhan the question Kyra most wanted to know.

Dubhan shook his head. "I knew of her family."

Kyra looked at Dubhan, and the moment his crimson eyes met hers, she knew she'd been silly to even think of being jealous. But in her defense, she'd never been in love before. She was crazy protective of Dubhan and their relationship—as new as it was.

Or maybe because it was so new.

Erith turned her head, causing a long, blue-black strand of hair to fall over her shoulder. "There are also the Warriors."

Once more, Kyra realized that there was so much more to the story than she knew. She'd been so wrapped up in all things Fae that she hadn't thought about anyone or anything else. That needed to change.

"The Warriors?" she asked.

Dubhan gave a nod of his head. "The strongest Celts of their family who allowed primeval gods to inhabit them so they could beat back Rome."

"Damn," Kyra murmured. Then in a louder voice, she said, "And these Warriors are still alive with these gods inside them?"

Erith answered. "Yes. They are friends of the Kings, and the Warriors also married Druids. Powerful Druids."

Death had said that the Kings had allies. Now, Kyra was beginning to think her idea was ludicrous. Apparently, with the friends the Kings had, they didn't need the Fae.

"I know what you're thinking," Dubhan said with a grin.

Kyra quirked a brow, then replied in a sassy, teasing voice, "You think so, huh?"

"You don't think the Kings need the Fae."

She glanced away. "Maybe you do know what I'm thinking."

"The Dragon Kings will need us," Dubhan stated.

Cael nodded. "He's right."

Death drew in a breath. "I'm going to visit the Kings and speak to Constantine about this."

"Are we joining the fight?" Dubhan asked.

Kyra held her breath as Erith and Cael exchanged a look. Then Death nodded once.

Dubhan smiled. "That's good. We need to be with them."

"You can thank Kyra," Erith replied.

Kyra was so surprised, she didn't know what to say.

"Don't be shocked," Cael said. "You said what needed to be heard, and in a way that made sense to everyone."

Erith took Cael's hand in hers. "This may not be my realm, but neither was the Fae Realm. Yet, where the Fae go, I follow. If this is their home, it needs to be protected. More importantly, the Fae need to remain allied with those whose home this is."

"The Dragon Kings," Kyra said.

Death faced Cael. They spoke quietly for a moment, and then she was gone.

Cael looked at them. "Erith will return later. I'll stay in case the Others decide to make themselves known."

"Kyra had another idea," Dubhan said.

Cael's brows shot up on his forehead. "Oh?"

"To talk to Mike—the mortal we sent into the bookstore—and perhaps get the book the girl had him buy."

"Hmm. That is a good idea."

Kyra grew uncomfortable at the praise. "It was both Dubhan's and mine."

"Take the compliment," Dubhan said as he wrapped an arm around her.

She rolled her eyes and smiled. "You're right. Thank you."

Cael chuckled and shook his head. "I'll be near, but not too close."

"Thank you," Dubhan said right before Cael raised his veil.

Kyra turned to him then. "What if all we're doing is the wrong thing?"

"What if it's the right thing?" he countered. "You need to trust yourself."

"This isn't deciding on what cut of meat to buy for dinner. There are millions of lives at stake."

Dubhan put his hands on her shoulders. "None of us are taking anything lightly, but you had good suggestions. Like I told Cael and Erith, sometimes, we're so bogged down by the fact there will be a battle that we don't see the forest for the trees. You saw what we couldn't. Maybe the Kings will go for it. Maybe they won't. Regardless, it's an option we should follow and see where it leads. It might be the one to save us all."

"I wasn't thinking about any of that when I spoke," Kyra said. "My only thought was that the Reapers should join the Kings. In fact, every Fae—Light and Dark—should join them, but they won't."

Dubhan shook his head. "No, they won't. Many will agree with the Others. For all we know, if we tell the Fae about the Others, some might join them, and we don't want that."

"You're right. Some Fae would join them. Some may already be trying."

"The Dragon Kings have never lost a battle."

Kyra gave him a flat look. "I'd disagree with that. Look who dominates this world—humans. And the Kings? They're hiding."

"The Kings didn't lose," Dubhan said. "They chose to stand down because of their vow to protect the mortals. There is a difference."

"I didn't think of it that way."

"There are always many sides to every story, and we never hear them all. But I've spent some time watching the Kings when I'm able. They're the best of us, the purest of us. The magic chose them, gave them this world to inhabit and make theirs. It was the Kings who were so welcoming, they invited the very ones who would ultimately destroy their lives into their home."

Kyra twisted her lips. "It's very sad. Are all the Kings so forgiving that they would live alongside humans?"

Dubhan threw back his head and laughed. "It's because Con is such a great King of Dragon Kings that he's been able to keep the others in line. And, trust me, all of them—even Con—have had thoughts of taking back their world."

"From all of us," Kyra said.

Dubhan nodded solemnly. "From all of us."

"I wouldn't blame them."

"Enough about the Kings. Shall we go see Mike?"

Kyra nodded. "Let's try calling him."

Several attempts later, it was obvious that Mike wasn't going to answer his phone. Dubhan took Kyra's hand, and in the next instant, they appeared at the library where Mike usually was.

Dubhan discreetly lowered his veil, and Kyra began asking if anyone knew where Mike lived. It didn't take long for someone to give them his address.

In the next heartbeat, they were outside the front door of Mike's flat.

Mike didn't open it when they knocked, however. He came to the door and demanded, "Who is it?"

"Dubhan and Kyra," Kyra said.

The sound of locks being turned reached them, and then the door opened. Mike looked at them and smiled. "I didn't expect to see either of you again."

"We wanted to see that you were safe," Dubhan said.

Kyra returned Mike's smile. "We tried to call you."

"Sorry about that," Mike said. "My mobile has been acting weird, so I tried to reset it."

"Weird how?" Dubhan asked.

Mike shrugged. "Just not working properly. And after . . . well, you know, I've been more paranoid than usual."

"Is that why you're in your flat and not at the library?" Kyra asked.

The mortal nodded and glanced at the floor. "It is."

Dubhan added, "We were wondering if we could have a look at that fiction book you bought?"

"Sure. Come in," Mike said and stepped back so they could enter.

The flat was sparse. The sofa had seen better days, as had the kitchen table and mismatched chairs, but the place was clean. Mike locked the doors behind them and walked around them as he went to the sofa where the book was opened and turned upside down. He picked it up, put in a torn piece of paper as a bookmark, and handed it to her.

"You've read over half of it," Kyra said.

Mike shrugged. "It's actually good. I didn't think I'd like fiction, but I do. Or at least I like this author."

"What's the book about?" Dubhan asked.

Mike lowered his gaze and shoved his hands into the front pockets of his jeans. "A Dark Fae who is trying to protect her people from this horrible group of dragons."

Kyra's stomach roiled. "Fae and dragons, huh?"

"It is a fantasy," Mike said as he met her gaze.

Dubhan caught Mike's eye. "I'm sure you've heard all kinds of Irish myths and legends."

"There are dozens of them, and yeah, my grandmother used to tell me all kinds," Mike said.

Kyra grinned. "My grandmother told me stories, too. I had my favorites. Which were yours?"

"Let's see," Mike said, his gaze going to an upper corner as he thought. "The Fae, probably."

Dubhan quietly asked, "And have you met any Fae?"

Mike suddenly became nervous as he shrugged. "Who can say?"

"You can," Kyra said as she caught his gaze.

Mike looked between the two of them, then did a double-take on Dubhan. When Kyra glanced at Dubhan, she noticed that he had removed the glamour to show his true coloring.

"You're Fae," Mike said, his voice holding surprise.

Dubhan nodded. "We both are."

CHAPTER

"What does that mean for me?" Mike asked.

Dubhan looked over the mortal for a moment and shrugged. "Nothing."

Mike made a sound, his face a mask of doubt. "I don't believe that. Beings like you don't tell humans such things without reason."

"It's because we trust you."

Dubhan didn't correct Kyra. In fact, they did trust Mike to some degree. Otherwise, they wouldn't have told him who they were.

Mike looked between the two of them. "In the book, it says there are two sects of Fae—Light, and Dark."

Dubhan had no idea that a book like that had been written, and if that little bit had been shared, what else was on those pages? "There are. I'm Dark. Kyra's Light."

Mike said nothing, but he was tense as if he no longer trusted them.

"Most mortals don't know about us," Kyra said. "There are some Halflings around—half-Fae, half-human."

"Yeah," Mike muttered, taking a little step back to put more distance between them.

Dubhan didn't have time for such things. "I'm going to put it bluntly. We could've killed you days ago if we wanted, but we didn't. We don't want to harm you. We had a business arrangement that went well, and you were paid handsomely for that."

"But you're here for something else," Mike said.

Kyra twisted her lips. "We'd like to read the book, and we'd like to know your thoughts on it."

Uncertainty filled Mike's eyes. "Why do you want to know what I think?"

"Because the girl gave it to you for a reason. To perhaps connect the dots of who we are," Kyra suggested.

Dubhan eyed the paperback in question. "The simple fact, Mike, is that we have enemies. The book could contain clues."

"So, the book was meant for you?" Mike said and answered his own question with a nod.

Kyra shrugged one shoulder. "Honestly, I believe the girl wanted you to read it, but we'd also like to see what's inside."

"She knew who you were." Mike blew out a breath. "I knew there was more going on than either of you told me, and I still think there's much more."

"There is," Dubhan replied. There was no sense lying to Mike, but that didn't mean Dubhan would tell him all of it.

Mike folded his arms over his chest and licked his lips. "Both of you have been fair to me. You gave me more money than agreed upon, especially for work that wasn't dangerous."

"I wouldn't say that," Kyra mumbled.

Mike paused, his gaze locking on her. Then he continued. "The girl was quite insistent that I read the book before passing it on to someone else who might be interested. I thought she liked me."

"She might." Dubhan shrugged. "She might have just wanted you to read the book."

Mike dropped his arms and ran a hand down his face. "I have to admit, it's a good book. I've been unable to put it down. I even skipped lunch."

"How about I get dinner, and you tell us what you've learned from the book so far?" Kyra suggested.

It took less than a heartbeat for Mike to agree. Dubhan remained silent as Kyra let the mortal pick what to eat. But if he thought Kyra was going to leave to get it, Dubhan was wrong. She snapped her fingers, and the food appeared on the table.

"Damn. I could get used to that," Mike said as he eyed the food, his stomach grumbling.

Dubhan might have had a harsh life, but he'd never gone without a meal. He jerked his chin to the table. "Eat. The discussion can wait."

"I can talk and eat at the same time," Mike said as he pulled out one of the chairs and sat, reaching for the first box that contained the Asian food he'd requested.

While he dug in, Dubhan looked at Kyra, who just grinned. In unison, they each sat in one of the chairs, their eyes on the human, who stuffed food into his mouth, chewing quickly.

"Sorry," Mike said around a mouthful of food. "As soon as I smelled it, I realized how famished I was."

Kyra shook her head, waving away his words. "No need to apologize."

After a few more bites, Mike slowed his eating. He took a long drink of water and said, "The book states that while to most, the Dark Fae are villains, they are, in fact, the saviors of the Fae."

"That's a first," Dubhan said.

Mike looked from Dubhan to Kyra and then back to Dubhan. "It also says that the Light and Dark don't commonly associate with each other."

"We don't," Kyra replied. "But Dubhan and I aren't exactly like most Fae."

"On the realm we once called home, the Light took one half, and the Dark the other," Dubhan said. "It's the same in Ireland. The Light took the top half, and the Dark the lower."

Kyra nodded slowly. "Dublin is the line that intersects the country."

Mike swallowed his bite of food. "All of that is said in the book. It also spoke about a civil war that caused your world to become inhabitable."

"Yes." Dubhan couldn't believe that their anger and hatred had come to that. But that's what happened when a race forgot that the realms weren't something to be plundered and eroded without consequence.

For the next ten minutes, Dubhan sat alongside Kyra as they listened to Mike explain the plot of the book in between bites. The heroine, a Dark Fae, saw the future for her people and knew that something had to be done. She aligned with other like-minded beings and created a group that set out to forge a different, better path.

"Does it say who the other beings were?" Kyra asked.

Mike shook his head. "Not yet. I get the feeling that isn't shared."

"Did a Dark really start all of this?" Dubhan asked Kyra.

Kyra met his gaze, her lips flattening briefly. "It's possible. I don't think we'll ever know who it was, though."

"Why not? If they're Fae, they may still be alive."

Kyra pondered that for a second and then nodded. "It's a long shot, but they could be. Are you telling me you want to find this Dark?"

"A female," Mike interjected.

"That could've been changed," Kyra told him.

Mike raised his brows and stared at her. "From what I've gathered of this book, it isn't fiction at all. It's a history of the Fae, marketed to humans as fiction."

Dubhan blinked, taken aback at that simple truth he hadn't realized until that moment. "I'll be damned."

"What?" Kyra asked, a deep frown on her brow.

Dubhan didn't answer her as he rose and went to get the book. When he returned, he took a closer look at the cover, especially the woman on the front. The model's face was semi-hidden, but upon closer inspection, he saw who it was.

He then held the book out to Kyra, whose frown deepened when he still refused to say anything. She finally snatched the book out of his hands and looked down. Seconds ticked by as she studied the cover. Then she gasped.

"I know," Dubhan said.

Kyra's silver gaze jerked to him. "I wouldn't have seen it had I not studied the woman."

"What are you two going on about?" Mike asked as he leaned his forearms on the table.

"We know who the book is about," Dubhan explained. "She's right there on the cover."

Mike pulled a face. "No kidding? You know this woman? She's real? Do you think I can meet her?"

Kyra gave him a harsh look. "You can't meet her. She's dead."

"Which means, we can't ask her anything," Dubhan said with a small shake of his head. Just when he'd discovered something that could help, it didn't do them any good.

"Dead?" Mike sat back, frowning. "From what I'm reading about her in the book, she's invincible. Not to mention the allies she has."

Unease rippled through Dubhan. "What do you mean she's invincible?"

"Invincible," Mike said, a bite to his tone. "What don't you understand about the word? It means she can't be killed."

Dubhan felt Kyra's gaze on him. She was thinking the same thing as he was—Usaeil's body had disappeared after Rhi killed her. All this time, Dubhan had assumed that Death had taken the queen but now. . . .

"I know that look on your faces." Mike swallowed hard and shook his head. "Something bad has happened."

"We need to read the book," Kyra told Dubhan.

While he agreed, a part of him didn't want to know what was between the pages of the story. He had a suspicion that whatever he learned would set everyone back on their heels.

Mike yanked the book from Kyra's hand. "Not until I'm finished."

Kyra held up her hands briefly. "I wouldn't dream of taking that from you before you were done."

"Good." Mike then flipped through the pages and found where he'd marked his spot.

Dubhan narrowed his gaze on the mortal. "Mike, did you record everything when you were in the bookshop?"

"No," the mortal said after a moment. "I shut off my phone when I left the store. Why?"

"Did the girl at the bookstore say anything to you that you

didn't quite understand? As if in another language maybe?" Dubhan probed.

"Now that you mention it, yes," Mike said as he looked up from the book. "Why?"

Kyra flashed a big smile. "No reason."

They fell quiet as Mike went back to reading, the food—and them—forgotten. Dubhan wanted to speak to Kyra, but out of earshot of the human, yet he didn't want to get too far away either. Dubhan jerked his head toward the door. Kyra nodded, and they rose quietly before making their way into the hallway.

"The Druid spelled him," Kyra said, her words laced with anger.

Dubhan waved away her words. "It's an inconvenience, yes, but no more than that."

"Depends on what else she did. For all we know, as soon as he finishes the book, he's going to join the Others."

"He's human. Why would they want him? He has no magic."

Kyra rolled her eyes. "You're the one with all the Dragon King knowledge, I can't believe you wouldn't piece together what the humans would do if they knew of the Kings now."

"Shite." Dubhan squeezed the bridge of his nose.

A moment later, Cael appeared. His face was lined with apprehension. "We have a problem."

"Just one?" Dubhan asked with a small laugh.

Cael didn't so much as crack a smile. Dubhan then took a closer look at the new god. Cael wasn't just concerned, tension gripped his body, and anger filled his dark purple gaze.

"Has something happened?" Kyra asked. "It isn't Erith, is it?"

Cael gave a single shake of his head. "She and the other Reapers are fine. It's what we've learned from Mike."

Dubhan waited, knowing that whatever words fell from Cael's lips would turn the tide of the entire situation. He wanted it to be in their favor, but it never was. Whatever Cael knew—and was about to share—was going to work against them. The question was, how much?

Cael drew in a deep breath before slowly releasing it. "We would've told all of you sooner had but one of you asked."

"Asked what?" Dubhan pressed.

"About Usaeil."

Kyra reached for Dubhan's hand, sliding her palm against his so their fingers interlaced.

"Death didn't take Usaeil's body," Cael announced. "We don't know where Usaeil is. Or who has her."

twenty-one

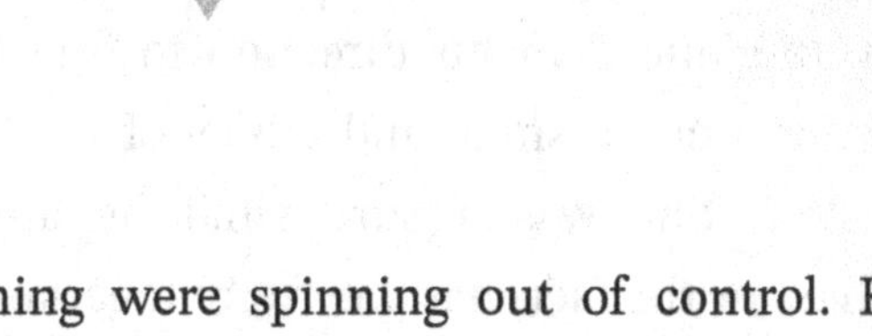

It felt as if everything were spinning out of control. Kyra waited for Cael to laugh and say that he was jesting, but he didn't seem the sort to joke—especially when it came to something so serious.

"Why didn't you or Death say anything?" Dubhan demanded.

Cael stared at him for a long time before he said, "Do you think she tells you every problem she's juggling?"

"I think what Dubhan meant to say was that this news is important, and while he understands that Death in no way owes anyone an explanation, Usaeil's body disappearing is something everything should know," Kyra said.

Dubhan held Cael's stony glare with one of his own. "Including the Dragon Kings."

"What Erith decides to tell Con and the Kings is her business," Cael replied.

Dubhan snorted. "You know exactly what Death will and won't share with everyone."

Cael shrugged one shoulder in response.

Kyra tightened her fingers around Dubhan's hand. His irritation wasn't getting them anywhere. "It doesn't do anyone any good for us to bicker among ourselves. This is a problem for sure, but one that can be worked out. Somehow," she finished, wondering why she couldn't seem to keep her mouth shut.

"Always the voice of reason," Dubhan said as he turned his head to her.

She looked at him, and to her surprise, his lips were turned up in a smile. She leaned forward and lifted her face, pressing her lips against his. Only then did she remember that Cael was there.

Kyra glanced in his direction to find Cael looking at her. He gave her a quick smile and a bow of his head as if to say that he approved. She wasn't sure what he approved of—her kissing Dubhan, or the fact that they were together.

Heck, for all she knew, it was both. Or something else entirely. It didn't matter. What she liked was that Cael appeared to accept her, which was all she needed.

"Kyra's right," Cael said. "Erith and I should've told all of you the moment we discovered that Usaeil was missing."

Dubhan looked at him and blew out a breath. "And I should trust that you and Death are handling everything as it should be."

"This is nice and all, but I'm confused," Kyra said. "From everything I've heard from other Fae, they saw Rhi plunge her sword into Usaeil. The queen is dead."

Cael quirked a brow. "Not according to what Mike said in there."

"There's something in the book," Dubhan said.

The three of them looked at each other. Cael veiled himself at the same time she and Dubhan walked back into the flat, but Mike was nowhere to be found.

"I knew it," Dubhan bit out.

Kyra released his hand and searched the tiny flat, hoping that Mike might be in the toilet or maybe hiding in the closet, but he was well and truly gone.

Cael appeared near the door. "There's something in that book the Others don't want us to know."

"I was sure the book was meant for us," Kyra said.

Dubhan stood with his hands clenched. "I think they wanted us to see it. I think they wanted us to figure out exactly what we did. We never should have left Mike alone."

"It wouldn't have mattered. He was going to leave with the book one way or another," Cael said.

Kyra happened to agree with the god/Reaper. She wasn't exactly sure what he was, but she knew he was powerful, in charge, and Death's lover.

"A Druid couldn't do this. Not up on the fifth floor," Dubhan pointed out.

Kyra walked to the window and looked out to the street below. "He got away somehow. There are no stairs here, but that doesn't mean magic was used."

She turned back around to see Cael moving his hand in a big circle before him as if he were wiping off a glass wall or something. As she watched, she actually saw his magic as trails of purple moving through the air behind his hand before they faded.

Then he halted his hand and closed his eyes. A moment later, shots of purple exploded out horizontally in all directions. There was nowhere for her to go, so she remained still and let the magic touch her.

The moment the power shot out, Cael's eyes opened, and he turned toward the table where they had left Mike reading. The food was just as it had been. Cael didn't touch any of it as he moved around Mike's chair.

"He was taken from this spot," Cael stated.

Kyra glanced at Dubhan, who merely shrugged his shoulders as if to say her guess was as good as his. Kyra was beginning to realize that Cael was quite new to this whole god thing, but whatever powers he had, they were impressive and extensive.

His purple eyes lifted and met hers. "Magic was used. Fae magic."

"Fek," Dubhan mumbled and turned away angrily.

Kyra couldn't pull her gaze away from Cael. "Why are you looking at me?"

"Because I get a sense of you here."

She jerked back, unsure if she'd heard him correctly. "I'm not a part of helping the Others. Not only did you see me in the hall, but you also know the Others are after me."

"Are they?" he asked.

Dubhan whirled around, his face set in hard lines as his red eyes glared daggers at Cael. "The Others were at her cottage. I heard them."

"But they didn't attack," Cael pointed out. "Both of you thought that was curious."

Kyra couldn't refute that. She glanced at Dubhan before she repeated, "I'm not helping the Others. You don't have to believe me, but I know the truth."

Dubhan came to stand beside her. He then took her hand in his and looked at Cael. "She's with us."

"I never said she wasn't," Cael replied. "I merely pointed out a fact."

Kyra didn't want to admit that he was right, but damn if Cael wasn't. She sighed and faced Dubhan. "I want you to know that I am with you. I have nothing to do with the Others, but I can see how it might look otherwise. I found you when no other Fae has been able to do that. I offered to help when most rational people wouldn't have. I came up with the idea that we should talk to Mike and read the book. And the most damning part is that Cael senses me in the magic."

"It's not you," Cael explained. "I sense a part of you. That's different."

A muscle ticked in Dubhan's jaw as he stared into her eyes. "I believe you. I know you. It sounds insane, but it's like I've always known you."

"Did either of you hear me?" Cael asked.

Kyra wanted to answer Cael, but her attention was on Dubhan. "I felt the same way the first time I saw you. It's why I tried to find you, and why I followed you when I finally did. Once I set eyes on you, I could think of nothing but getting close to you."

"Like our souls had found each other once more."

She grinned, nodding. "Yes."

There was a long, drawn-out sigh from Cael.

Dubhan finally turned his head to the god. "I've never sensed anyone's magic like you just did. How do you know it isn't Kyra?"

"For one because, like she said, she was with us. I suppose she could have a twin, but I believe that what I felt of her would've been stronger."

Kyra looked between the two men. "I still don't understand what that means."

"Family," Cael said. "It means that I felt just enough of you to know that it's someone who's part of your bloodline. Someone in your family was here."

As if she hadn't been shocked enough the past few days to last a lifetime. Kyra had no response. What could she say?

"How do we find out who it is?" Dubhan asked.

Cael twisted his lips. "Only I can. I'll know it when I feel that person's magic. Dubhan, don't leave Kyra's side for a second. Forget Mike. He's out of our reach now anyway."

"What about the book?" Kyra asked. "There has to be another copy somewhere. We could look for that."

Cael nodded. "Be careful where you go."

"What are you doing?" Dubhan asked.

"I'm going to pay a visit to Kyra's family."

Her lips parted to mention her aunt, but she didn't get any words out before Cale disappeared.

"It's going to be okay," Dubhan said.

She looked up at him. "Is it? My family is involved with the Others."

He gave her a wry look. "So is mine."

"I'm sorry. You're right. I was feeling sorry for myself, but I shouldn't. We shouldn't," she corrected. "Neither of us is responsible for what our family does. We make our own choices, and those are the ones we're responsible for."

"Will you still feel the same way when Cael returns and tells you which of your family members took Mike?"

"I hope I do, but if I don't, remind me."

Dubhan flashed her a smile. "I will, but only if you do the same for me."

"Promise," she said. "Now, let's turn our minds to something we can do. Like finding another copy of that book."

He chuckled. "You really do have to occupy your mind all the time."

Dubhan used his magic to produce a computer where they looked up the title of the book to find another edition. It pulled up immediately, but they couldn't seem to find an available copy anywhere. There were no new ones printed, and all the used copies had been purchased.

"It's not coincidence," Dubhan said.

Kyra sighed loudly. "No, it isn't. Someone doesn't want us to read that book."

"I suspect because there is something in there that could help us."

"Then why put it in the book?"

Dubhan shook his head as he snorted. "Hell if I know."

"That would be the one thing I'd be sure to omit."

"It would make sense." Dubhan rubbed his chin thoughtfully. "What if Usaeil didn't write the book?"

Kyra considered that for a moment. "Why wouldn't she? It is about her. She's even on the cover."

"What if someone else did? Say a Druid who heard the stories. What if they took one of the photos of Usaeil when she was posing as an actress and manipulated it enough to create the cover?"

"I suppose any and all of that is possible."

"Then wouldn't it stand to reason that the books were a way to pass down the information to other Druid members of the Others? Or even those who might wish to join?"

Kyra had to admit, it seemed plausible. "If Usaeil had written the book, she wouldn't have been able to keep it to herself."

"Not with her being on the cover. She paraded as an actress," he exclaimed. "She loved attention. She wouldn't have passed up the opportunity to tell everyone about this."

"We may never find another copy of the book. Even if we found the author, I'm not sure what good it would do."

Dubhan shook his head slowly. "It wouldn't."

"What do we do, then? Because I can't stand around waiting for something to happen."

He pulled her into his arms. She blinked, and they were back in her cottage. He said nothing as he held her.

"Not that I don't like this, but what are we doing?" she asked.

"We can't find Xaneth. We lost Mike. There isn't a copy of the book available for sale. And the Others are after us. I say we get naked so I can lick you from head to toe."

She shivered and looked up at him. "Hmmm. That sounds very appealing."

"You still have your clothes on."

"I do."

He glanced at the ceiling in frustration. "You have an idea."

"There is someone who might either know how to get a copy of the book or might know the secret in it."

Dubhan's lips flattened in a line. "Maximillian."

"Max," Kyra replied with a nod.

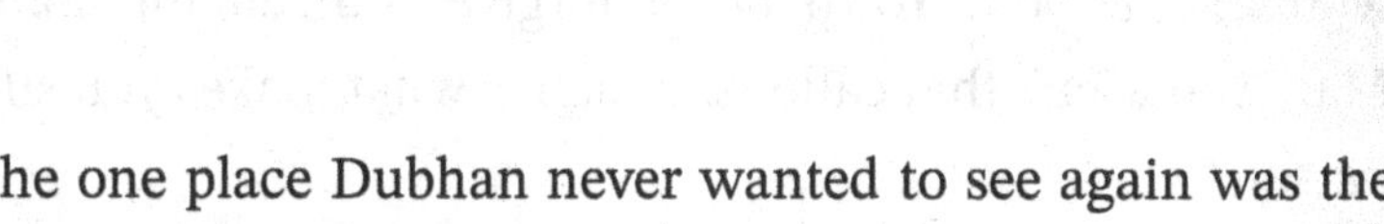

The one place Dubhan never wanted to see again was the one place he had to visit.

"Are you sure about this?" Kyra asked for the third time.

Dubhan wasn't sure at all, but it wasn't as if he had a choice. "I'll be fine."

"You passed out before. I'm not even sure how you managed to stay with me the entire time."

He shrugged, thinking of the symbol Max had used to keep Reapers out. Dubhan had still been able to get into Max's place, but it hadn't been easy—or fun. In fact, the pain that bombarded him had made it difficult to concentrate on everything that had been said.

"Max knew you were there," Kyra said.

Dubhan looked into her silver eyes. He didn't want to discuss her ex-lover or the man who had helped his family betray him. Dubhan would rather take his time having sex with Kyra.

"You aren't going alone," he stated.

Kyra rolled her eyes. "I don't expect to. I have a simpler plan. I'll just remove the symbol on the outside of the doorway."

"I don't know which one it is."

She shrugged. "It doesn't matter. I'll remove them all."

"Then you leave Max open to his enemies."

"He made them, not me."

Dubhan eyed her for a long moment. "You'll essentially be sentencing him to death, you know that, right?"

"I know."

Her words might be strong, but he heard the hesitation in her voice. "Even if it were possible for you to remove the symbols, I wouldn't let you. You'd never forgive yourself for doing that to Max. You aren't that callous, which is what makes you such a good person."

"There has to be a way to remove the symbols. I've heard whispers about it being done."

"Only the one who put up the symbols can remove them."

She waved away his words. "I know. I've heard that my entire life, but things happen. Fae die, which means that someone has to be able to erase the markings if they want."

She had a point, but he'd really hoped that she wouldn't think of it. "Kyra, please. Don't do this."

"Why not?"

"I went with you before. I can do it again."

She shot him a dry look. "Do you really think Max is going to believe I had someone with me and not reinforce those symbols?"

Dammit. Dubhan looked away, his options were running out quickly.

"I can do this," Kyra insisted. "I can remove the symbol, and

I'll be fine with whatever the outcome is for Max because this is for you, for me, and for all Fae."

He pulled her into his arms and held her, squeezing his eyes closed. If only he could erase the symbol, but since he was one of those being kept out, he couldn't touch it.

Kyra pulled out of his arms, but she linked her fingers with his. With a quick smile, they teleported to the top floor of the building. But as they approached the turn in the corridor that would take them to the hidden Fae door, the hairs on the back of Dubhan's neck stood on end. It was the only warning he got to let him know that they weren't alone.

He wrapped his arms around Kyra, bringing her back against his chest as he raised his veil right before they turned the corner. The moment he saw the other eight Fae, he put his hand over Kyra's mouth.

They stood as silent as the dead. None of them spoke as they stared at the place he and Kyra were. It was as if the Fae knew that they had been about to arrive. But that wasn't possible.

The minutes ticked by. Dubhan had an itch on his ear, but he didn't move. He knew for a fact that no one would be able to see him, but he wasn't going to take the chance. The slightest sound could set off those around him.

The Fae—both Dark and Light—were armed for battle. The Dark stuck together, as did the Light, but they were communicating through hand signals.

Twenty minutes later, a tall Dark male stepped forward. His hair was slicked back in a pompadour style with the sides shaved. He held out his arm before him, his palm facing out. A moment later, a male Light joined him, mimicking the pose.

Dubhan watched them, wondering what they were doing. Then, he lifted Kyra and took a step back around the corner just as magic came barreling down the corridor. The edges of it singed him, alerting him that the Fae had used a spell to detect if someone was near but hiding.

Another five minutes went by without Dubhan moving his back from the wall. Kyra didn't so much as twitch. Her breathing was even, and her hands gripped his arm, her fingers tightening occasionally.

Finally, Dubhan leaned around the corner and studied the hallway. All the Fae were gone. No one could use a veil and not be seen by a Reaper. Then again, these weren't just any Fae, that much was clear. He suspected they could be part of the Others. Or maybe they were a new enemy altogether.

He set Kyra down and removed his hand from her mouth as he turned her to face him. He put a finger to his lips. She nodded in response. With one hand still on her to ensure that she remained veiled, Dubhan kneeled down and spread his fingers wide. With a push, he sent magic out of his palm and down the corridor to see if they were alone.

They were, but Dubhan wasn't sure when or if the Fae would be back. He stood, and with hurried steps, they both stalked to the Fae doorway. Dubhan paused when he saw that several symbols had been burned off while one had just been scraped through with a blade of some sort. Which made it appear as if Max had been visited by two different sets of people who weren't fond of his symbols.

"Everything okay?" Kyra whispered as she glanced over her shoulder.

Dubhan felt what was left of the scraped symbol and immediately jerked back. That was the one to keep Reapers out, which meant that Death or one of the other Reapers had been there already. Dubhan gave a nod and walked through the Fae doorway.

Kyra's gasp of dismay stopped him cold. There wasn't much left of Max's place. Everything had been destroyed. There wasn't a trace of the Fae anywhere, but Dubhan wasn't surprised. It was only a matter of time before Max received what had been coming to him. No being in the universe could dole out the things Max did and not have it come back around on them eventually. Honestly, with Max, it had taken far longer than Dubhan would've thought.

He didn't believe a Reaper had done this. If one of his brethren had been there, it was to get information, not to tear up the place. Death could have judged Max, but again, there was no reason to destroy the flat. Which meant that it must have been whoever those other Fae were.

Dubhan didn't release his hold on Kyra. He wasn't certain there wasn't someone—or even a spell—that would alert others that they were there. Being veiled prevented most spells from detecting a Reaper.

Most.

Everything was in question now because of the Others. The Fae that had been there when they arrived could be a part of the Others—or they could be something else.

Dubhan gave a little yank on Kyra's hand. She nodded, turning toward him. The moment they exited the Fae doorway, he teleported them to four different locations before he stopped.

"Those Fae were waiting for us. How did they know we would be there?" Kyra asked.

Dubhan looked around the vast Avondale Forest Park before he lowered himself to a fallen tree. "I thought they expected us, and perhaps they did, but I think they knew we'd be back to visit Max. Not when we were coming."

"Either way, I don't like it."

He pulled her down beside him and put his arm around her. "Neither do I."

"Your quick-thinking saved us."

"When you're in as many of those types of situations as I've been in over the course of my life, you learn to pick up on little things that warn you."

"And something warned you?" she asked, her head turning to him.

He nodded.

"I'm glad it did." She swallowed and looked toward a bird that swooped down from a tree to grab a worm. "Max is dead."

"It looked that way."

"Did the Others do it? Or the Fae that were there? Or are they one and the same?"

Dubhan shrugged. "The Others might have done it. And I don't know who those Fae were, so I can't tell you if they are a part of the Others or not. I do know a Reaper was there at some point because I was able to walk through without pain. It would be just like Erith to send a Reaper to Max's."

"Wouldn't the Reaper have still been there?"

"I would've left after Max was killed." Dubhan was thinking of who it might have been when Cathal appeared before them. "Cathal."

The Reaper was the tallest of them, his red eyes penetrating. His long, black and silver hair hung midway down his back. "I arrived back at Maximillian's just as the two of you left."

"Arrived back?" Dubhan asked.

Cathal's nostrils flared. "I followed the other group of Fae."

"Who were they?"

"I don't know, but they were powerful. Very powerful," Cathal said. He ran a hand down his face. "I've not seen that kind of power in a Fae since Usaeil or Rhi."

Kyra licked her lips. "And Max? Is he dead?"

Cathal nodded once. "It was the group of Fae. I removed the Reaper symbol so I could get into Max's. I was there to watch and see if I could learn anything more about the other symbol or the Others. Then the Fae showed up."

"Did they want something from Max?" Dubhan asked.

Cathal snorted. "Nothing. They didn't even speak. They stormed in, and when Max tried to teleport, they caught him with a net."

That took Dubhan aback. "A net?"

"It looked as if it was made of silver. It stopped him." Cathal glanced at the ground. "I'll give it to Max. He didn't beg them for mercy. Even when they began cutting him to pieces."

Kyra sucked in a breath and covered her mouth with her hand.

Dubhan held her close and nodded at Cathal. "Thanks for telling us."

"I'll see you soon," Cathal said and nodded to both before vanishing.

Kyra shook her head. "I'm sorry Max is gone. It was a horrible death, but at the same time, he didn't live a good life."

"You die how you live. I know that for a fact."

Her gaze softened. "Yes, you do."

"We don't have the book, or even know where to locate it," he pointed out.

She placed her hand atop his. "We'll find it."

"You have such confidence."

"I have to. This is too important."

He smiled and kissed her temple while his thoughts remained on the group of Fae. If they were enough to cause a Reaper to think them powerful, then they were someone the Reapers needed to learn about. And quickly.

But Dubhan kept that to himself. Kyra had enough to deal with. If only Dubhan could give her some closure on her aunt, but there hadn't been time to do anything about that yet. But he would find a way.

"Where are we?" she asked.

"Avondale Forest in Ireland. I wanted to be sure we weren't followed by an enemy."

They sat in silence for a few minutes, each lost in thought. Dubhan had yet to let his guard down. There was too much about the Others that he didn't know or fully understand yet, but he wasn't going to underestimate them.

Then there was Usaeil. How was the queen not dead? There were so many unanswered questions, and Dubhan wasn't sure he wanted to know the answers. The odds weren't in their favor, but that was usually the way of things.

Everything had been stacked against them with Bran, and yet they had defeated him. The Reapers would do the same to the Others. But this time, the Reapers wouldn't be alone. They would be standing alongside the Dragon Kings.

"Ready?" Dubhan asked Kyra.

As soon as she nodded, he took them back to the cottage. Once inside, he tested the spells he'd put up to ensure that no one but a Reaper or Death had gotten inside while they were gone. All was as it should be.

Why then did he still get the feeling that there was more coming? Dubhan couldn't put his finger on it. He checked every room of the small cottage twice, double and triple-checked the wards and spells. Yet that niggling feeling that something was about to happen wouldn't dissipate.

"You're freaking me out," Kyra told him as she sipped tea, standing and leaning against the kitchen counter.

He blew out a breath. Maybe it was all in his head. After the run-in with the Fae at Max's and the Others seemingly all around them, Dubhan could be seeing things that weren't there. He was that protective of Kyra. But it was better to be wary than not.

Dubhan turned his head to her and smiled. "I'm just being precautious."

But she wasn't looking at him. Kyra's face was slack, her lips slightly parted as shock widened her eyes. Her fingers loosened, and the cup tumbled from her hand to plummet to the floor where an explosion of porcelain and tea followed.

"Eva," she murmured.

Dubhan frowned, then looked over his shoulder in the direction of Kyra's gaze. That's when he saw the woman standing outside the house.

Before he could warn Kyra not to leave the cottage, she had teleported outside. Dubhan immediately followed. He stood behind her, his gaze locked on the woman who resembled the love of his life.

"Kyra," the female said.

Kyra started to take a step forward, but then stopped. "Eva. Where have you been? I've looked for you for years."

Dubhan used his magic to feel behind and around him to see if anyone else was near. Thankfully, it was just Eva. But that didn't mean the Fae wasn't deadly. He could hardly believe he was staring at the aunt Kyra had told him about, the one Kyra assumed was dead.

Because the woman before him was very much alive.

She had the same wavy, black hair as Kyra, the same shaped

eyes, and even the same height. It was almost like Eva was Kyra's twin, that's how closely the two resembled each other.

Dubhan noticed Eva's dark denim-encased legs and the black biker boots on her feet. She had a black moto leather jacket on with a white tee beneath. Her hair was down, and there was no sign of any jewelry.

Eva twisted her lips. "I had business I needed to see to."

"Business? You just left me," Kyra stated, anger tinting her voice.

Dubhan remained near Kyra. He wanted to feel joy for Kyra at Eva returning, but he couldn't shake the feeling that something wasn't right.

Eva shrugged. "Duty called."

The moment she said that, Dubhan's gaze narrowed. His Reaper senses picked up movement in the air. Out of his peripheral vision, he spotted Cael, Eoghan, Aisling, and Rordan arrive with their veils raised.

"Duty?" Kyra repeated. "What duty?"

"The same duty I've come to collect you for."

Kyra shook her head. "I'm not going anywhere until you tell me what you're talking about."

"A group of people who are doing whatever is necessary to make us the great race we once were," Eva explained. "The best of us get chosen. I'm going to make sure I'm chosen, and if I can't, then you will be."

"Others," Kyra said, revulsion contorting her face and deepening her voice. "You're referring to the Others."

Eva sighed and shook her head sadly. "I see you've already made your decision. That's too bad." Her gaze briefly met Dubhan's.

Kyra moved back to stand even with Dubhan. "I spent years

looking for you, asking everyone I knew where to find you. How could you just walk away without a word to any of us? To me?"

It killed Dubhan to hear the hurt in Kyra's voice. He wanted to give her vengeance, but he didn't move. Not yet. Not when there was more to learn about the Others or the other mysterious group, if there was one.

When Eva didn't answer, Kyra crossed her arms over her chest. "You need to leave. Now."

Eva made a sound as she slowly shook her head. "You have two options, Kyra. You can join us, or you can die. We need your powers. I've been watching you for some time. I'm the one who made sure you were stuck in the shield at the Light Castle so you could the Trackers. I had no idea the Reapers were real or that you'd fall for one, but that's fine, too. We need more information on them."

"You aren't touching Kyra," Dubhan stated.

Eva smiled. "Try and stop me."

"Oh, we will," Dubhan replied.

CHAPTER

CHAPTER
twenty-three

It all happened so fast. Kyra's mind was still reeling at the sight of her aunt, then learning the reason she hadn't been able to find Eva was because her aunt had become part of the Others —or was trying to. Or was part of another nefarious group. But all of that paled in comparison to when she told Kyra that she would die if she didn't join, as well.

Kyra heard Dubhan's threat, but it sounded as if she were in a tunnel. She blinked, unsure of what to do. Her aunt, the same one who had taken her in, loved her and showed her how to be herself while being a part of their family was now going to kill her. Something didn't make sense.

"You just had to go poking your nose in our business," Eva said to Dubhan. "And you got Kyra involved. I should've told her about the Others long ago when I could've swayed her."

Kyra didn't like being talked about as if she weren't there. "I wouldn't have joined you even then."

"It was freeing being able to finally share the secret I carried for so long—that I'm Kyra's mum," Eva said, ignoring Kyra.

Kyra felt as if she'd been kicked while she was down. "Stop it."

Eva's silver eyes slid to her. "You seriously never figured it out? Why do you think your parents allowed me to step in when I did? Why do you think I contacted you after not having anything to do with you growing up?"

"Enough," Kyra said with a shake of her head.

"No, it's time you heard the truth. My lover was part of our group before he was killed. He was married, and I was young. I didn't want to raise a child, so my father suggested I give you to my brother and his wife to raise since they had already begun their family. It seemed perfect. And it was. Until you showed signs of being just like me." Eva shrugged. "You can try and deny that you aren't part of this group, but the magic runs in your veins, blood from both your parents. You can't stop destiny."

Kyra drew in a shaky breath. "The hell I can't. I know what's right and wrong, even if you don't. This realm isn't ours. We were allowed to live here, and we certainly have no right to take it from the Dragon Kings. I will be standing against you."

Eva smiled. "No, child, you won't. You'll be dead. And there's nothing this Reaper can do to stop me."

"We'll see about that," Dubhan said.

Kyra thought back to all the times she could've learned some combat skills in case of an attack, but she was absolutely defenseless. If it weren't for Dubhan, she knew she wouldn't stand a chance. She didn't want to be that powerless and weak, and if she survived this, that was going to change.

Eva rolled her eyes at Dubhan. "Did you really think I'd come to face a Reaper and not be prepared?"

"Did you really think I'd bring Kyra and not be prepared?" Dubhan asked with a sly grin.

Eva's confidence slipped, showing enough uncertainty to make Kyra smile. This woman who she had loved—and even wished had been her mother—couldn't be the woman who birthed her. But so much made sense now.

Had Eva been this woman all along, and Kyra was only now seeing it because her aunt—er . . . her mum—was finally showing her true colors? It was all just too much.

"I'm not afraid of you," Eva told Dubhan. "I've been watching you."

Kyra glanced at Dubhan, but he didn't seem at all fazed by what was being said.

"Is that so?" he replied. "What did you find out?"

Eva snorted. "You think I'm going to tell you?"

"It doesn't matter what you did or didn't see."

Kyra knew that Dubhan was referring to the rule of the Reapers. Did that mean that Death was there? The other Reapers? Had they come to kill Eva? A part of Kyra wanted to stop them. Then she looked at her aunt/mother and realized that if Eva returned to her group, she would do so with more knowledge of the Reapers.

That simply couldn't happen.

"You used me," Kyra said. The words falling from her lips before she even realized it. She looked at Eva and shook her head. "You used me from the beginning."

Eva's nostrils flared as she shook her head. "Not at first. I wanted to help you, to show you there was another path. But you're too much like your father. You see good in everything without seeing the opposite side. You didn't listen to me, so I left, making sure to keep tabs on you. Imagine my surprise when you were at the Light Castle when Usaeil sent her Trackers. I was just as shocked as you to discover the Reapers."

"You were there with me?" Kyra asked in confusion.

Eva flashed a smile. "Oh, yes. I saw the entire glorious battle."

Kyra looked at Dubhan. She didn't need to ask him to know that other Reapers were there and that they planned to kill Eva. Kyra grabbed Dubhan's hand, and while their palms touched, she called forth a knife.

Dubhan's brow furrowed. "Kyra," he began.

She gave a slight shake of her head.

"Between the ribs on the left side," he whispered.

She swallowed and turned to her aunt. Kyra kept the blade hidden against her forearm as she released Dubhan's hand and took a step toward Eva.

"I'm your daughter, but you said you'll kill me if I don't join you."

Eva nodded. "Those are the rules. Bloodlines are important to the Others. Especially ours."

"There are many of you, then?"

"Nice try," Eva said with a laugh. "As if I'd tell you that."

"I know it began with two Fae and two Druids."

Eva looked skyward and vacillated for a moment. "There were six in the main group of Others."

Damn. Kyra had wanted information, though she hadn't thought she would get anything. It wasn't much, but at this point, anything was better than nothing. She slowly kept moving toward Eva. "You want me to join a group you won't tell me anything about."

"You've already said you want no part in it." Eva glanced at Dubhan. "In fact, your lover has made it clear he intends to try and kill me."

"Can you blame him? You did threaten my life," Kyra pointed out.

Eva chuckled. "I suppose I'd do the same in his shoes."

"You were the one who killed Tate and Jesta."

"I didn't deal the killing blow," Eva stated with a shrug. "I did pay them a visit, telling them I was your mum and warned them against you, as well as threatened their livelihood. I thought it would be enough. Then you were seen going into the shop. It didn't take much . . . prodding . . . to get Tate to tell me everything you talked about. Once I was done, they were killed."

Kyra swallowed. She'd known in her gut that Eva had been responsible, but hearing it made it so . . . real. "And Max?"

Eva's smile was slow. "He did his best to talk his way out of it, but it was futile. He knew we were there because of you."

That was like a punch in the gut.

Kyra couldn't understand the woman before her. She was the exact opposite of the aunt who had spent years with her, sharing tubs of ice cream, watching the tele, telling stupid jokes, and urging Kyra to do everything without magic.

"Why did you do all the little things like mortals, telling me not to do magic all the time?" Kyra demanded to know.

Eva rolled her eyes. "Let me guess, you're still doing things like the humans." She threw back her head and laughed. "You have no idea the strength of your magic, Kyra. If only I'd gotten the Kavanaugh power instead of you. I could be using it for the Others instead of watching you waste it."

"What?"

"You use it without even realizing it. You want to help anyone and everyone, even animals," Eva stated, her voice growing louder. "That kind of power should be used for something more important than healing a bird's broken wing. That's why I kept urging you not to use your magic. You were wasting it."

Kyra stopped walking since she now stood within inches of Eva. She looked into the woman's silver eyes and found a stranger staring back at her. The best years of her life had been with her aunt, and yet they had all been a lie.

Kyra didn't care about that. She'd learned a lot of valuable things that had helped her forge a solid path. No matter the lies, no matter the reasons, Kyra was stronger because of everything.

"You shouldn't have gotten so close to me," Eva told her.

Kyra's throat tightened with emotion. She swallowed it and said, "I had no choice."

Out of the corner of her eye, Kyra saw Eva's arm lift as an orb of magic formed. Kyra saw the determination in Eva's eyes. There was only one path for her. Without hesitation, she thrust the blade between the Fae's ribs and right into her heart. Her motions were so smooth, Eva felt nothing.

"You aren't even scared," Eva said with a laugh.

Kyra took a step back, pulling the knife out as she did. Blood dripped onto the ground. Eva's gaze lowered to the weapon before she looked down at herself. It was only then that she comprehended what had happened. She clutched at the wound, but it was too late. Her legs wobbled before giving out. By the time she hit the ground, she was dead. Seconds later, she turned to ash.

Kyra stared down at her. She'd never taken another person's life before. It felt . . . horrible, no matter the reasons behind it. She'd thought of Eva as her savior for so long. It would've been easier to let Dubhan or one of the other Reapers take her aunt/mother's life, but she couldn't do that. This was her family, her responsibility.

Something warm and solid wrapped around her hand. She

looked down and saw Dubhan's fingers. He gently took the weapon from her and then turned her to face him. His strong arms wound around her as he held her. She stood there for a moment, holding onto him with all that she had. She didn't understand why he was holding her. Seconds ticked by, and then the tears came.

After she'd cried buckets for taking what she now knew was her mother's life, her guts roiled. She turned away, emptying her stomach while Dubhan held her hair out of her face. When she finished, he gave her water to rinse her mouth and a towel to wipe her face. Then he held her once more. He said nothing, simply gave her comfort with his touch. She was glad for it because she couldn't stand to hear any words at the moment. Not when her mind was still coming to terms with the fact that she had killed a woman she had loved and admired.

She didn't know how long they stood there before she felt strong enough to lean back and look up at her Reaper. He wiped away the remnants of her tears before taking her into the cottage. He took off her clothes and put her into bed before he stripped and climbed beneath the covers with her.

They lay on their sides, her back to his chest as they looked out the window at the sun sinking into the horizon. Everything had changed that day. And, oddly enough, it felt as if her slate had been wiped clean. As if she got to decide what the next step was.

But she'd already made that decision. It was—and always would be—Dubhan.

twenty-four

The feel of a soft hand caressing his chest pulled Dubhan from his dreams. He smiled when Kyra's lips kissed along his cheek and then down his jaw. They had spent the night making love, holding each other, talking, and then making love again. It had been the best night of his life. Even better, he knew that it was the start of something truly amazing, and he couldn't believe that Kyra had actually come into his life.

He groaned when her hand wrapped around his hard cock. "Woman, haven't you already had enough?" he teased.

She chuckled, her warm breath fanning his neck. "Of you? Never."

He had her on her back in a blink. Dubhan looked down at her as he felt their love surrounding them. "Perfect answer."

"And you?" she asked, brow quirked as she continued stroking his arousal. "Haven't you had enough?"

"I'll never get enough of you. Not in a hundred lifetimes."

She smiled, love shining in her eyes. "I'm so glad we found each other."

"Me, too, love." He lowered himself so he could kiss her.

Their embrace became passionate as the desire surged within them again. He couldn't get enough of her body, her quick mind, or her sensual nature. He loved how, when they spoke of the future, she included him. And he couldn't wait for her to meet the other Reapers.

Her legs parted as she brought his cock toward her entrance, but they both stilled when they heard someone clear their throat from the other room.

Dubhan dropped his forehead against hers. "I think our time is up for the moment."

"For the moment," she whispered and gave his rod another stroke before releasing him.

He moved off her to lean on one elbow but couldn't stop looking at her as she rose from the bed and began dressing. Of all the people in the universe, he'd never thought he would know what love was. He'd never expected it to find him, never even dared dream that something so beautiful and wonderful could be his.

Kyra looked at him over her shoulder after she'd tugged on her shirt. She flipped out her hair that was still in its natural state. After flashing him a bright smile, she gave him a wink. "Come on, handsome. We need to get moving."

As he rose, he called his clothes to him. By the time he was on his feet, he was fully dressed. "I'm waiting on you, beautiful."

She laughed, shaking her head. After slipping on some shoes and running her fingers through her hair, she gave him a nod. They walked from her room together to find Eoghan standing in the kitchen, making some tea.

He glanced their way. "Morning. I left you alone as long as I could."

"Thank you," Kyra said. "Need some help?"

Eoghan shook his head. "You two sit. I've got this."

Dubhan waited until Kyra had taken a chair before he also sank into one. Many things were running through Dubhan's mind, but he kept silent, waiting to see what Eoghan would say. And he didn't have long to wait.

"Kyra, what you did yesterday was more than anyone expected of you. Especially Death." Eoghan faced them with a tray in his hand. He walked to the table and set the tray down before filling three cups with tea and handing each of them a mug. Only then did he sit, his gaze going to Kyra.

She glanced down at the tea and shrugged. "It had to be me."

Dubhan reached over and covered her hand with his. They hadn't spoken of what had happened to Eva once during the night. He'd planned to let her bring it up when she wanted to because he knew how hard it was for her. No matter how she looked at it, she would carry that weight around for the rest of her life.

But she was strong enough not to succumb to the weight of it. Dubhan would make sure he helped her if she stumbled, though he doubted that would ever happen.

"You did what you felt you had to," Eoghan said with a nod. "You showed your true character yesterday, but none of us were surprised by it. You don't hesitate to stand up for what you believe in, and that isn't something many can claim."

Kyra met Dubhan's gaze before her head turned to Eoghan. "You heard Eva. Both of my parents are part of those trying to get to be an Other."

"So?" Dubhan said. "My entire family is. What matters is what you do."

Eoghan nodded. "I agree with Dubhan. We can't help what our family does or the decisions they make. The only thing we can control is our choices. You made yours yesterday."

"Actually," she said as she smiled at Dubhan, "I made that decision well before that."

Dubhan grinned like a fool while tightening his hand on Kyra's. He'd never been so happy.

"Yes, I can see that," Eoghan said, a smile in his voice before he took a drink of tea.

Dubhan pinned Eoghan with a look as he began to worry about Eoghan's appearance. "Why are you here? I thought Death already approved of Kyra."

"Erith has," Eoghan replied calmly, setting his cup down. "I'm here to let you know that we need to be especially watchful now that the Others know of us. We don't know what that means for us going forward. But at the very least, they know of one group of Reapers."

"No matter how hard they look, they won't find anything on any of you," Kyra said.

Eoghan blew out a breath and sat back in the chair. "We can't assume anything. We don't know if Usaeil is alive or dead. No doubt she told them enough when we had our run-in with her."

"Usaeil has known about us for some time," Dubhan pointed out. "She could've told the Others, or at least the group Eva belonged to, at any time, but based on what Eva said, they only recently found out about us."

Kyra wrinkled her nose. "I'm not sure I'd believe too much of what my aunt said."

"I agree," Eoghan stated. "Regardless, neither of you should stay on this realm for long."

Kyra made a sound in the back of her throat. "There's nowhere else to go."

"Actually, there is," Dubhan said and brought her hand to his lips to kiss her knuckles.

Eoghan got to his feet. "Thanks to Kyra, Erith is talking to the Dragon Kings about joining forces."

"Should it take so long?" Kyra asked. "I figured it would be a quick discussion."

Dubhan shrugged. "There is nothing simple about two powerful forces joining."

"Until that time comes, we need to be more careful where we go and who we interact with," Eoghan told him.

Dubhan saw the wisdom in such a move. "What about Xaneth?"

"We will continue looking for him. Erith isn't going to give up so easily on finding him after everything he did for us. I'd like to think we'll find Xaneth soon, but I don't know. The Others need to be dealt with, and I believe it'll happen much sooner than we think." Eoghan rose to his feet. "I expect to see you both shortly."

No sooner were the words out of his mouth than he was gone.

Dubhan pushed away his untouched cup of tea and focused on Kyra. He started to open his mouth when her finger touched his lips to silence him.

"Should we speak?" she asked, a frown marring her forehead as she dropped her arm. "What if the Others are listening?"

"They can't hear us. I made sure of that. Nor can they get into this cottage. We're safe, for now, but I wouldn't want to stay for much longer."

Kyra nodded slowly. "Okay. Where do we go?"

"We have a place. It was Death's, actually, but she opened it to the Reapers."

"And she's letting me come?"

"Of course," he said with a smile. "You're part of me now."

Her mouth split into a grin. "I am, aren't I? And I like the sound of that."

"Will you be all right leaving all of this behind? You won't be able to tell your family anything about us."

She licked her lips and looked at the table. "I don't speak to them much, and it's not like I'd really know what to say now anyway. I can't tell them about Eva. They'd never forgive me."

"There's nothing to forgive," he reminded her. "She was going to kill you. You protected yourself."

"My family might not see it that way."

"Or they could."

She lifted one shoulder. "It'll be some time before I want to find out one way or another. It's all still so . . . raw."

Dubhan tugged her arm and pulled her into his lap. "There is no rush. We don't even have to discuss it ever again. You tell me when and if you're ready."

"I love you," she said.

He gave her a soft kiss. "I love you."

"And I really get to see where you live?"

"It's where we're going to live."

Kyra opened her mouth to speak, then closed it, letting out a breath.

"What?" he urged. "Tell me."

"I'm just wondering what my role will be."

Dubhan looked into her silver eyes and felt such love that he was overcome with it. "You'll be mine. And I'll be yours. Forever. You can do as much or as little as you want."

"I'm not one for sitting on the sidelines."

"I'll support you in whatever you want to do."

She looked away briefly. "That's good to know, but I was talking about us initially."

"Us, how?" He suspected he knew where she was going with this, but it wasn't something he'd planned to talk to her about until later.

For the first time, he saw her uncertainty when she looked at him, and he didn't like it.

Kyra drew in a quick breath. "I don't expect anything. I want you to know that. I just like to know what I'm going into. I plan to be with you always, but—"

"You wish to know what you'll be called."

"Yes," she replied with a quick smile. "Exactly that."

He tugged on a strand of her hair. "Well, there are a few Reapers who have gone through the marriage ceremony. Others who are simply together but haven't done the ceremony yet."

"I see."

"What would you rather?"

Kyra's lifted one shoulder in a shrug. "I . . . I don't know. I'm not against the ceremony, but I'm not exactly for it either. I guess as long as I know we're together, that's enough for me."

Dubhan held out his hand, and once she placed hers in his, he held it against his heart. "How about we make our own vows, and if we ever want the official ceremony, then we can do it?"

"You mean, like our own private ceremony?" she asked, her eyes bright with excitement.

"Yes."

She smiled, nodding. "I like that."

"I vow to you that I will love you until my dying breath and beyond. I will honor, trust, and respect you. I will stand beside you in all things and will gladly shoulder anything you can't carry. I will protect you in all ways."

Kyra's eyes shone bright with unshed tears as she moved their hands to cover her heart. "I give you my oath that I will love you from this life into the next. I will honor, trust, and respect you. I will stand beside you always, and I will shoulder anything you can't carry. And I will protect you in all ways."

"I am yours," he said. "And you are mine."

A tear slipped down her cheek as she smiled. "I am yours, and you are mine."

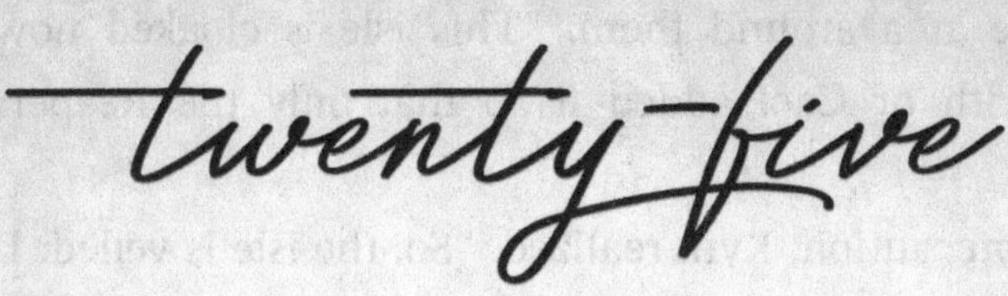

twenty-five

Kyra didn't think twice about the cottage or her motorbiker as she held Dubhan's hand, and he teleported them to a small isle in the middle of a lake.

She looked around. "Where are we?"

"Scotland," he answered. "I'll show you how to get here, but for now, I want you safe."

"The Others aren't around."

He raised a black brow. "How do you know?"

"I'm guessing by the tight way you're holding onto my hand that we're veiled."

Dubhan nodded once.

"No one can see us," she said.

He glanced out over the dark blue waters, and angry clouds gathered overhead, heavy with an approaching storm. "I just found you. I won't lose you so soon. I might be overreacting, but I'd rather be safe than sorry."

"You're right. We don't know the extent of the Others' power. So, why test it?"

He gave her a brief smile, worry still in his crimson eyes as he scanned the area around them. "This isle is cloaked now. I'm guessing Erith or Cael added it so that only the Reapers can find it."

A wise precaution, Kyra realized. "So, the isle is veiled. Do we need to be?"

He didn't release her hand, which was her answer. Dubhan closed his eyes, his brow furrowed. "There are also several layers of spells and wards. Certain names have been added to allow entry on the isle now." His red eyes opened, and he looked at her.

"I know very little about Erith, but she doesn't seem the kind that does anything by half-measures. She'll protect her Reapers at all costs."

Dubhan loosened his grip and gave her a side-eye while grinning. "Your name is added with the others."

It was just another way the Reapers and Death were letting her know that she was one of them. Her side might not win in the coming battle, but there was no other place she'd rather be. Not just because she knew it was the correct side to take a stand with, but because of the love she'd found with Dubhan.

"Ready?" he asked as he faced the doorway.

Kyra gazed at the Fae doorway and then looked at him. "Yes."

With one step, she was transported to another world. It was so beautiful that she was at a loss for words. Her senses were assaulted by flowers of all sizes and colors, the birds singing around her, and the light perfume of the flora.

She didn't have time to investigate the area because Dubhan was pulling her after him. They weaved through the various flowers and plants while she smiled as a dragonfly zipped around her, the buzzing of its wings causing her hair to move as it got close.

The world smelled so fresh, so clean that she couldn't stop taking in deep breaths. Then they were out of the garden, and she spotted the white tower gleaming in the cloudless sky.

"Welcome to Death's realm," Dubhan said proudly.

He was staring at the tower, but Kyra was looking at him. "Isn't it your world now, too?"

"I suppose." He looked at her then. "But in my mind, this will always be Death's."

Kyra jerked her head toward the tower. "I'm guessing that's where Erith and Cael live."

"It is. She opened up the entire realm to us Reapers and has allowed us to find whatever spot we want to build our homes."

The idea excited Kyra. "We can choose any place on the realm?"

"Uh-huh."

"Have you explored it all?"

He shook his head, a grin pulling at his lips.

She looked around in the distance at the mountains on one side and a thick forest on the other. "In which direction do we look first?"

"Whichever one pleases you."

Her head swung back to him and then she faced him, moving her arms up his chest and then around his neck. "I want us to choose the place together."

"We will."

She narrowed her eyes and cocked her head to the side. "Will you really tell me what you like? Or will you wait for me to say I really like something and then choose that?"

"Possibly the second option. I'm happy if you're happy."

How could she be irritated with that logic? "I accept that, but if there's a place you really don't like, or one that you do, will you tell me?"

"I promise."

"Then that's all I need to know."

His lips flattened as regret pulled at his face. "I wish we had time to explore the realm at our leisure."

"Don't," she told him. "It's something we can look forward to after this business with the Others is taken care of. Until then, wherever we are together is home for me."

"You are quite something, Kyra Kavanaugh."

She rose up on her tiptoes and lifted her face for a kiss. He had just barely touched his lips to hers when he sighed. Kyra opened her eyes and then looked behind her to see a row of Light and Dark Fae as well as several Halflings staring at them. Off to the side, Eoghan stood with a woman who bore a faint resemblance to Usaeil.

They were surrounded immediately. Kyra listened as some of the Reapers teased Dubhan about his smile since it wasn't something they were used to seeing. Then, all eyes turned to her.

Kyra tried to remember all the names of the Reapers in Dubhan's team as well as those that Cael led. Then there were the women with the Reapers. One by one, they came and spoke until only Eoghan, his woman, and Aisling remained.

Eoghan and the Halfling approached first. "Kyra, I'd like for you to meet Thea. She is Usaeil's only surviving child."

"Not for dear old Mum's lack of trying to kill me," Thea said with a laugh. "It's good to meet you, Kyra. I've heard a lot about you the last few days."

Kyra nodded, her mind still absorbing the fact that Usaeil had a child, which meant that Thea had a claim to the throne. "It's good to meet you, as well."

"I see the wheels turning in your head," Eoghan told Kyra. "Trust me, Thea wants no part of the throne."

"Heavens, no," Thea said with a shake of her head.

There were another few minutes of pleasantries where Kyra noticed several characteristics of Usaeil in Thea. Kyra wasn't sure the Halfling knew, so she wasn't going to point it out. Kyra wouldn't want to know such a thing, especially if her mother had tried to kill her.

But wait, Eva had. That was something she and Thea had in common. No doubt they'd talk about that at length later. Maybe then, Kyra would get to hear the whole story about how Usaeil had tried and failed to kill her own daughter.

Once Eoghan and Thea walked away, a petite Reaper with blood-red nails and her black and silver hair in various braids walked up.

"Dubhan," she said.

"Aisling," he replied.

Aisling then turned her deep red eyes to Kyra. "If you ever want to talk about what happened yesterday with your mum, I'll be around."

And with that, she walked away.

Kyra turned to Dubhan. "What was that about?"

"I don't know," he said with a shrug as he watched Aisling. "We're all private about our pasts. Death was there with all of us, and she made sure that Eoghan knew so he could help his group if we needed it, but we've not shared among ourselves." He slid his gaze to Kyra. "I can tell you that Aisling doesn't offer up things like that. Ever."

Kyra turned to look at Aisling's retreating back. "That was her way of welcoming me. She wouldn't have said that if she didn't know exactly what I was going through."

"That's what I think, as well." Dubhan's arm went around her.

Kyra couldn't wait to get to know Aisling better. There was something in the female Dark's eyes that spoke of intense pain, well hidden. Kyra recognized it because that had been her at one time. Maybe it was again after Eva, but she had Dubhan now. And an extended family that no one in their right mind would ever cross.

"I don't know how much time we have before Death and Cael return," Dubhan said. "We can start investigating the realm."

"Or?" she asked when he trailed off.

He shrugged and smiled down at her. "I was just thinking we might finish what Eoghan interrupted this morning."

Kyra looked at the sky and thought about that for half a second. "I'm going with option two."

"I was hoping you'd say that."

"Mountains or the beach?" he asked.

She shrugged, her blood heating as desire surged. "I don't care as long as we aren't interrupted for at least an hour."

He said nothing as he smiled and teleported them away. Kyra suddenly found herself next to a river deep in the woods. There was a large cave that Dubhan turned toward. He led her to it, and as they approached, a huge bed appeared. This time, Kyra didn't hesitate to use her magic to remove their clothes.

Dubhan looked down at his naked body and then smiled at her. He lifted her in his arms and stalked to the bed. Their lips were locked by the time he laid her on the thick mattress.

She sighed as his hands roamed over her before moving between her legs and stroking her sex. The world fell away as Kyra succumbed to the expert touch of Dubhan's hands, lips, and tongue.

This was the start of her new life.

This was the beginning of a future with her Reaper, her love.

Her Dubhan.

Epilogue

Death stared out over her realm. Cael came up beside her. She'd never thought much about the things she'd had to do as either Death or the Mistress of War. But with Cael beside her helping her, there was no denying the weight he'd taken from her, allowing her to breathe easier.

"You made the right call," he said.

She leaned her head against his arm. "You knew all along we'd be joining the fight against the Others, didn't you?"

"Yes," he said without hesitation. He moved his arm, wrapping it around her. "I was waiting for you to come to that realization yourself. And I knew you would."

"Why didn't you say anything?"

He chuckled. "You weren't ready to hear it."

"I still wasn't ready to hear it, especially from Kyra." Erith blew out a breath. "But I'm glad it was said. It gives us some time to prepare."

"So it begins," he said.

She lifted her chin. "So it begins."

Cathal sat before a fire, sharpening the blade of his sword. He liked the open plains so he could see in all directions around him. No enemy could sneak up on him out here. It was nothing but an endless sea of grass swaying in the breeze with the sky meeting it on the horizon.

Every Reaper was made for war. Some might not admit it, but he knew what he was. It was time the Others discovered that, as well.

He didn't care who made up the secret group, or if they were one or many factions. The fact that they were rising up against the Dragon Kings and the Reapers was enough for him. Had the Others not turned their sights on the Reapers, he still would've gladly fought with the Kings against them.

Cathal had lost one world. He wasn't going to lose another.

Thank you for reading **DARK ALPHA'S TEMPTATION**.
I hope you enjoyed the story as much as I loved writing it.

If you want more Reapers, then you're in luck!
Up next is **DARK ALPHA'S CARESS**.

BUY DARK ALPHA'S CARESS NOW
at www.DonnaGrant.com

✦

And don't miss out on the Dark Kings series.
The next book set in Dark Universe, is **DRAGON LOST** …

BUY DRAGON LOST NOW
at www.DonnaGrant.com

✦

To find out when new books release
SIGN UP FOR MY NEWSLETTER today at
https://www.tinyurl.com/DonnaGrantNews

Join my Facebook group, Donna Grant Groupies, for exclusive
giveaways and sneak peeks of future books.
https://bit.ly/DGGroupies

✦

Keep reading for a peek of DARK ALPHA'S CARESS and a
glimpse at DRAGON LOST …

SNEAK PEEK AT DARK ALPHA'S CARESS
REAPER SERIES, BOOK 10

I am a Reaper—an elite assassin bound to Death.

I follow the command. I take the mark. Nothing stops me.

Not even the darkness that finally dragged me under.

I should have been lost to it forever.

But one sound pulled me back —her music.

Thea is a Half-Fae, cautious yet fierce, and her music awakens a hunger I've never allowed myself to feel.

Every note pulls me closer.

Every breath around her tests the control I swore never to break.

Her melodies cut through the void, and pull me into the light, leading me back to my brethren…and into a rising war. Whoever hunts her may be the key to uncovering the enemy stalking us all.

For her, I'll shatter my vow of silence.

For her, I'll face the shadows still clinging to my soul.

For her…

I'll risk everything.

New York Times and USA Today bestselling author Donna Grant delivers a dark, sensual tale of danger, desire, and the love powerful enough to pull even a Reaper from the edge.

BUY DARK ALPHA'S CARESS TODAY
at www.DonnaGrant.com

Ballycastle, Ireland
July

She had officially lost her mind. That was the only thing she could think of that would have taken her from her home on the Isle of Skye and brought her to Northern Ireland. Sorcha wasn't exactly courageous. In fact, she considered herself a hermit.

But because she preferred to be alone, it made it easier for her to do precisely what she was currently doing.

"Rhona, you owe me big for this," she mumbled to herself as she walked the hilly landscape toward the coast.

The wind whipped her hair from its braid and into her eyes. She pulled the strands out of her lashes and tucked them behind her ears, but it did no good as the next gust tugged them free and put them right back.

Sorcha's heart pounded more erratically with every step she

took. She was the last person who should be here. She was a horrible liar. Not only that, but she also caved under pressure. Always. There was a reason she liked her solitude. She didn't have to answer to anyone, and no one looked to her for anything.

Which meant she couldn't let anyone down.

But this was bigger than her. It was bigger than the Skye Druids. That's why she was here. No longer could she turn a blind eye to what was going on. What Usaeil had done to Corann, the leader of the Skye Druids, was enough to convince Sorcha to get off her arse.

It had been no surprise when Sorcha learned that Rhona had taken over as leader of the Druids. As soon as she heard the news, she went to Rhona and offered to do anything to help. It'd never entered her mind that Rhona might send her off on a dangerous mission that could very well get her killed.

Sorcha stopped walking. Her thighs burned from the incline. The sky had grown darker from an incoming storm. She turned and looked back the way she'd come. There hadn't been anyone around, and that's how this had been planned. The only way this would work was if she remained unseen. Even so, she and Rhona had come up with a story in case she *was* stopped.

She drew in a deep breath and zipped up her raincoat. Every fiber of her being wanted to return to Skye and the safety of her cottage. For so long, she had buried her head in the sand and let others handle things. All because she was too scared to actually live.

Bracing herself for whatever was to come, Sorcha began walking again. The climb up to the summit was for skilled climbers only. Spray from the sea coated everything in a fine mist, making the rocks and the grass slippery. She had to watch every step she took. And she wasn't even to the most dangerous part yet.

Climbing such cliffs and mountains had been something Sorcha had grown up doing with her mother and sister. She was an expert, but that didn't mean she liked what was happening. She didn't know these cliffs like she did the ones on Skye.

A crack of lightning followed closely by a boom of thunder made her jump. Loose sediment slipped beneath her feet and caused her to slide. She quickly grabbed hold of an outcropping of rock and a clump of grass to stop herself.

"Bloody hell," she murmured and paused long enough to gather herself.

Then she continued. She didn't look back again. Little by little, she progressed over the terrain. She covered a lot of ground before the first raindrop landed on her. Sorcha ignored it as the path became narrower. She glanced up and saw a group of people ahead. The moment she saw them, she ducked down, afraid that they might have seen her, as well.

When no shout of warning or the sound of anyone coming for her followed, Sorcha slowly rose up enough to see ahead. Only then did she continue on. The fat raindrops came down more readily. She lifted up the hood of her raincoat as she inched closer, using the footholds and handholds to keep herself anchored to the cliff. Then—finally—she was there.

Sorcha pressed her forehead to the damp rocks of the cliff and let out a relieved breath. She'd worry about getting back once she was finished here. She strained her ears to listen, but she couldn't make out any of the words being said by the group. She had come this far. There was no way she would leave without something.

She reached up and grabbed a rock before she set her foot on another and climbed. It was only a meter's difference, but it allowed her to hear. The only problem was that she needed to hang off the side of the cliff to do it.

"...you have to see," a woman said, her Irish accent thick. "Now is our time. We can no longer stand back and wait for someone to come to us. It's time *we* act."

A man snorted loudly. "We might be Druids, but we do not stand a chance against the Fae. I've heard they're gathering their own group."

"Fek the Fae," the woman stated angrily. "This isn't their world. It's ours!"

A cheer went up from the others.

"You say that until a Fae shows up," the man retorted. "I doubt you'd be so quick to say those words if they did."

Sorcha raised up enough to try and see who had spoken. The crowd stood in a circle. A glow emanated from the ground in the center of the group, the light showing everyone's face, including the man and woman in the middle. The woman was in her mid-forties with chin-length straight, black hair laced with gray. She was attractive with a trim figure she showed off with tight-fitting clothes.

The man appeared his forties, as well. He was tall with broad shoulders and a beer belly that looked as if he'd sported it for many years. His blond hair had thinned on the top, and the comb-over he seemed to prefer, blew in the wind.

Sorcha knew that the Fae sometimes liked to use glamour to disguise their beauty so they could walk among mortals. There was always a chance there could be Fae around, but she didn't think the two main speakers were it. The fact that she was hiding proved just how secretive this meeting was. And how secure the area had been.

None of them seemed concerned with the cliffs, because only someone highly skilled—or an idiot—would even dare what she was doing.

Sorcha was pretty sure she was also an idiot, but there was no turning back now. She was here, and she would finish her mission so she could return with intel for the Druids. Then, she would go back to her cottage and return to the hermit lifestyle she'd lived for the past decade.

The woman in the middle of the circle shook her head. "Patrick, isn't it time we stood up to the Fae? Isn't it time we showed everyone who we are?"

"We?" Patrick asked with a bark of laughter. "You can combine all of our magic together, and it still wouldn't be enough against *one* Fae. How the bloody hell do you think we can fight against them?"

"Who said anything about fighting them?" she asked with a pointed look.

Patrick ran a hand down his face and walked away a few steps before turning back to her. "You've lost your mind. You're basing all of this on hearsay."

"Hearsay from someone who is a Fae," she pointed out.

"Beth, that Fae could've been planted at the pub so you'd overhear him and do all of this."

"You heard him, too."

Patrick sighed as he dropped his chin to his chest and put his hands on his hips. After a few tense moments where the only sound was the rain pelting the ground, he lifted his head. "The Others were disbanded. Whatever their main goal was, we'll never know. But what we do know is that they're gone."

"There's no way they're gone," Beth said.

There were nods of agreement from the other Druids around the circle, some adding "ayes," as well.

Sorcha's arms started to ache. She wasn't sure how much longer she could stay in this position.

"It was probably all a lie," Patrick said.

A woman with dark skin stepped forward. "It isn't a lie. I can say that because I was part of the Others. Moreann chose me herself."

Everyone looked at the woman, including Sorcha. She memorized the woman's features, all while hoping to hear a name.

Beth gave Patrick an I-told-you-so expression. "Between her words and what we overheard, I decided to call this rally together with those I knew were not only powerful enough to stand against the Fae but also strong enough mentally to know what they're getting into."

Patrick ignored Beth and looked at the other woman. "Where is Moreann?"

"I don't know. I've not heard from her in weeks."

Patrick threw up his hands and glared at Beth. "See?"

"But..." the woman said, drawing out the word to get everyone's attention. "I can tell you that I was visited by the Dragon Kings, who made it very clear that I was to forget anything to do with the Others."

At the mention of the Dragon Kings, some Druids stepped back, visibly shaken, while others frowned in concern. Sorcha knew of the Kings, but she had never met one. She honestly wasn't sure she wanted to. She knew they protected this realm and had since the beginning of time, but they were obviously a group that one simply didn't want to fuck with on any level.

Beth jerked her head to the woman. "Dragon Kings? You never said anything about them."

"Why does it matter?" the woman asked with a twist of her lips.

"It matters because of who they are," Patrick told her. "You should take their warning to heart."

The woman laughed. "The Others were out to destroy the Kings. And it was working, too."

Patrick rolled his eyes. "Obviously not if the Others are gone, and the Kings are still here. And why would the Others want to be rid of the Kings?"

"None of that matters!" Beth shouted and slashed her arm through the air to halt any more talk. "We're here because the Others needed Druids. That's what we are. If the Fae think they can form a group themselves to take over what the Others began, then there's no reason we can't do the same."

This time, it was Sorcha who rolled her eyes. She debated showing herself to the group to tell them the facts of what had happened between the Others, the Dragon Kings, the Fae, and the Druids. Still, she realized none of them would believe her. They wanted their own version of the facts, and that was the only thing they would listen to. It would be her folly if she allowed them to know that she was here.

No longer able to hold herself up, she let her arms straighten so she could lower herself down. It didn't take long for her to realize that the words of the group were garbled once more. Sorcha steeled herself and resumed the position to pull herself up.

"We need to take a vote," Patrick said.

Beth nodded and folded her arms over her chest. "I agree. All for creating a Druid group, raise your hand."

Sorcha's gaze scanned the circle to see that more than half had raised their hands.

"Against?" Patrick asked as he raised his.

Fewer people were completely against the idea, but even more in the circle hadn't chosen a side at all.

Beth flashed a bright smile. "Guess we know who wins."

"Not so quick," Patrick pointed out. "Many didn't vote."

Beth wasn't happy to hear that. She must have realized that if she pushed things now, those who didn't vote might not side with her, which meant that Patrick would have won. Instead, the Druid said, "All right. Let's take a few days to think about it. Let's meet back here again in three days. Everyone who comes must vote. Understood?"

The group nodded and began to turn and hurry away as lightning lit up the sky. With that cue, the rain intensified. Sorcha wanted to stay and listen, see if anything else was exchanged. But between her arms aching and the roar of the rain, she doubted she'd be able to hear anything. Deciding to be safe, she carefully lowered herself and looked over her shoulder at the storm that raged behind her.

She then looked at the cliffside and the narrow trail she'd used. The growing darkness, along with the storm, made it difficult to see. She didn't want to get caught out on the cliffs. It was either go up and climb over the edge with the possibility of someone in the group seeing her. Or she could go back the way she'd come.

Sorcha debated the choices for a moment and decided to chance going back along the cliffs. This wouldn't be the first time she'd gotten caught in a rainstorm while climbing. But it was the first time in Ireland on cliffs she didn't know. And, she was alone. Without anchors.

"Well, this night just keeps getting better and better," she said.

She took a step and was suddenly slammed against the cliffs by a fierce wind gust. Her hands clenched the rock in an effort to stay rooted to the spot. Maybe she should've chanced climbing up and over. Then she thought about being caught climbing up with wind like that, and it sent a chill down her spine.

"Slow and steady," she told herself. The same words her mother had used often with her and her sister.

The rain pelted her now. The droplets were large and heavy as they slammed against her. The lightning, wind, and thunder sounded and felt as if it were on top of her, but she didn't look up to find out. She didn't take her eyes from her route, because all it would take was one slip for her to fall. No one would hear her screams over the storm, and her body would likely not be found for days.

She had no identification on her, so the authorities wouldn't even be able to return her to Scotland. The last thing she wanted was to die in Ireland. She still couldn't believe she was on the isle the Fae called home. She'd hated it for as long as she could remember, and the current situation didn't make her feel all warm and fuzzy.

An eternity later—with a couple of heart-stopping slips—she finally made it back to solid ground. Even then, she had to traverse the rocky terrain down to where she'd parked the rental car.

Sorcha picked up the pace. Now that she was off the cliffside, she felt she could move more quickly. It was a mistake. Within minutes, her foot slipped off a wet rock, and she twisted her ankle. She crumpled, grabbing her injury.

"Dammit," she said as her ankle began to throb.

Out of the corner of her eye, she spotted lightning not far from her. It hit the ground, causing a loud crack. Sorcha screamed and jumped. She had to get to the car and out of the storm. She wasn't safe here. But when she tried to put weight on her injured foot, her eyes welled up with tears.

She fell back onto her butt and slapped her hand on the ground beside her. How could this be happening? She knew better than to rush through terrain she didn't know, but to do it at twilight during a storm? It was a rookie mistake that she shouldn't have made.

Lightning flashed again, revealing the outline of a man about twenty meters below her. He stood as still as a statue as he faced her. She jumped for a second time, unsure what to do. Was it one of the men from the rally? Someone else?

The man moved slowly toward her before he stopped again. Another flash of lightning revealed his very tall silhouette and incredibly broad shoulders and thick arms showcased by his wet tee shirt that was now molded to his body. She couldn't see much of his face other than a strong jawline and penetrating eyes.

"You seem to be in need of assistance," he said.

She heard the Irish accent in his deep voice. He purposefully kept his distance so as not to scare her. The next flash of lightning had him looking up at the storm above them.

"I think we'd best get out of this weather, don't you?" he asked as he offered her his hand.

There was no way she could get down to her car without help. She had no choice but to trust him. "Yes," she said and took his proffered palm.

He easily lifted her into his arms, cradling her against him. Sorcha felt the movement of his muscles beneath her hands as she wrapped them around his neck. There was no denying the hard stomach against her. Or the softness of the long hair he had gathered at the back of his neck.

There was something about a man with long hair that just did it for her. Few could really pull it off, but she gave credit to those who tried.

Within moments, they were at the bottom of the mountain not far from where she'd hidden her car. She glanced back at the rugged terrain, trying to figure out how he'd come down it so quickly. Had she been so wrapped up in all the hard sinew against her that she hadn't paid attention? There was no other explanation.

"Where shall I take you?"

Her head snapped toward his. That's when she realized that she was very near his face. Unfortunately, she still couldn't get a good look at him. "Oh. Um...my car is parked over there," she said, pointing in the general direction.

He said nothing else as he strode to her vehicle. Once there, he gently set her down until she leaned against the car with her injured foot lifted.

"Thank you," she said.

He gave a nod. "You should be careful. These are dangerous times, and there are many more dangers out there."

She couldn't tell if he was threatening her or warning her, not that it mattered. She was well aware of what was out there. Sorcha pulled the key fob from her pants' pocket and unlocked the vehicle. "You're very right." She opened the car door. "Thank you a—"

But when she glanced up, he was gone. Sorcha didn't look for him. Instead, she got into the car and locked the doors before starting the engine.

BUY DARK ALPHA'S CARESS NOW
at www.DonnaGrant.com

GLIMPSE AT THE NEXT DARK UNIVERSE BOOK

DRAGON LOST, DARK KINGS, BOOK 16.5

From *New York Times* and *USA Today* bestselling author Donna Grant comes a new story in her Dark Kings series…

Destinies can't be ignored. No one knows that better than Annita. For as long as she can remember, it's been foretold she would find a dragon. A real-life dragon. She's beginning to think it was all some kind of mistake until she's swimming in one of the many caves around the island and discovers none other than a dragon. There is no fear as she approaches, utterly transfixed at the sight of the creature. Then he shifts into the shape of a thoroughly gorgeous man who spears her with bright blue eyes. In that instant, she knows her destiny has arrived. And the dragon holds the key to everything.

All Royden wanted was to find an item his brother buried when they were children. It was supposed to be a quick and simple trip, but he should've known nothing would be easy with enemies like the Dragon Kings have. Royden has no choice but to trust the beguiling woman who tempts him like no other. And in doing so, they unleash a love so strong, so pure that nothing can hold it back.

BUY DRAGON LOST TODAY
at www.DonnaGrant.com

ABOUT THE AUTHOR

New York Times and *USA Today* bestselling author Donna Grant® has been praised for her "totally addictive" and "unique and sensual" stories.

She's written more than one hundred novels spanning multiple genres of romance including the bestselling Dragon Kings® series that features a thrilling combination of Druids, Fae, and immortal Highlanders who are dark, dangerous, and irresistible. She lives in Texas with her dog and a cat.

www.DonnaGrant.com
www.MotherofDragonsBooks.com

facebook.com/AuthorDonnaGrant
instagram.com/dgauthor
tiktok.com/@donnagrant_author
bookbub.com/authors/donna-grant
goodreads.com/donna_grant
pinterest.com/donnagrant1